A Killer Watches . . .

The man frowned as he saw Inspector Reed and Clint Adams together in the lobby of the hotel. They did not look like a policeman and someone who was under suspicion for murder. They looked too friendly.

Suddenly the man didn't find Clint Adams so interesting anymore.

Suddenly he saw Adams as a threat—an even more threatening figure than the inspector. At least the man understood policemen.

He did not understand legends of the American West at all.

But that didn't mean he couldn't kill one. . . .

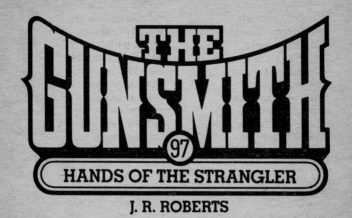

THE GUNSMITH

97

HANDS OF THE STRANGLER

J. R. ROBERTS

JOVE BOOKS, NEW YORK

THE GUNSMITH #97: HANDS OF THE STRANGLER

A Jove Book/published by arrangement with
the author

PRINTING HISTORY
Jove edition/January 1990

ISBN: 0-515-10215-6

Jove Books are published by The Berkley Publishing Group,
200 Madison Avenue, New York, New York 10016.
The name "JOVE" and the "J" logo
are trademarks belonging to Jove Publications, Inc.

PRINTED IN THE UNITED STATES OF AMERICA

10 9 8 7 6 5 4 3 2 1

ONE

"I'm always sticking my nose where it doesn't belong," Clint Adams said. His tone of voice made it clear that this was meant as a lament.

"That's called helping people," Rick Hartman said.

"That's called being nosy," Clint said, "and I've made an art form of it."

"Is that a fact?"

"Yes," Clint said firmly. "It is."

Clint Adams and Rick Hartman were in Hartman's saloon, the largest in the town of Labyrinth, Texas. Clint had returned from a rather arduous experience the week before and had been following this particular line of conversation ever since then.

"Clint, ask any of the people you've helped over the years what they think."

"I'm not talking about them, Rick."

"Then what *are* you talking about?" Rick asked. "Or should I say, who?"

"Me," Clint said. "I'm talking about me."

"All right," Rick said with a sigh. "I'll bite. What about you?"

"I should do something for myself for once."

1

"Didn't you do something for yourself when you went to Australia?"

"Sure," Clint said, "and look at what I got involved with down there. No, I want to do something for myself and keep my nose out of other people's business while I'm doing it."

"Impossible!"

"What do you mean, impossible?" Clint demanded.

"Just what I said," Rick replied. "It can't be done."

"Would you like to bet on that?"

Rick laughed and said, "Anytime."

"You're so damned sure of this, huh?" Clint asked, showing some degree of annoyance.

"Look," Rick said. "Don't get sore—"

"I'm not sore!"

"You're *getting* sore," Rick said.

"All right," Clint said. "I'm calm now. Explain yourself."

"What's there to explain?" Rick asked. "I believe that you crave other people's troubles."

"Oh, come on—"

"No, look at the record. Wherever you go, if there's someone who needs help, you offer your help —and I'm not saying that's bad. In fact, I think it's very good for you and for the people you help."

"This is all your opinion."

"Of course it is."

"Well, I'm done with it, then."

"No you're not," Rick said. "You're just a little

tired and maybe a little depressed. You need a vacation."

"Isn't that what I've been saying?"

"But even on vacation," Rick said, "if you see someone who needs help—"

"I'll run the other way."

Rick smiled and said, "I repeat—impossible!"

"And I repeat," Clint said. "Do you want to bet?"

"Yes!"

"How much?"

"Wait a minute," Rick said, holding up his hand. "Let's define the bet first."

"All right, go ahead," said Clint.

"I bet that no matter where you go for your vacation, you'll end up offering to help someone with their problem—and you'll probably get yourself in hot water doing it."

"That's the bet?"

"Yes," Rick said. "But I'll even pin it down more precisely than that."

"How?"

"The person you help will be a woman."

"And that's the bet?"

"That's the bet."

"Done!" Clint said. "How much?"

"A hundred dollars."

"Making it easy on yourself, huh?"

"All right," Rick said. "Five hundred dollars, and if you lose, you work as bartender for me for two weeks."

"And if I win?"

"Name it."

Clint stopped a moment, then said, "I can't think of anything right now."

"That's all right," Rick said magnanimously. "Name it when the time comes."

"An open-ended bet?" Clint asked. "You're *that* sure?"

"Clint," Rick said, "I know you. Putting a damsel in distress in front of you is like waving a red flag at a bull. You can't resist!"

"You have a bet, my friend," Clint said, extending his hand. "And I'm warning you, it's going to cost you dearly."

"We'll see," Rick said. "Now, where will you be going on your vacation?"

"I don't know," Clint said.

"Well, pick a place," Rick said, "in, say, the next three days."

"All right," Clint said.

"The bet starts when you get there."

"And runs how long?"

"Whenever you get back."

"No time limit?"

"As short or as long a time as you want—within reason, of course."

"Sure," Clint said, "the longer the better for you."

"All right, let's pin it down," Rick said. "No shorter than a week."

"And no longer than a month."

"Done!"

"Done and done!"

• • •

The bet was made, and suddenly Clint was uncomfortable. Rick was playing the odds, and they were in his favor. Clint couldn't remember the last time he'd walked away from someone—especially a woman—in trouble. He was going to have to change that now. Not for the money or the servitude behind Rick's bar. No, he was going to have to change it for his own peace of mind.

He was going to have to buck the odds—but then, that's what being a gambler was all about.

TWO

Three days later Clint was in bed with Chloe—one of Rick's newer saloon girls—in his hotel room. Chloe was a blonde in her early thirties who was a little more serious minded than most of the girls Rick hired for his saloon. That stemmed from the fact that she was also a little older than most of the others. When Clint had arrived in Labyrinth this time, he'd been in the mood for someone mature, someone he could talk to. Chloe—despite her parents' unfortunate choice of first names—fit that bill perfectly.

It didn't hurt that physically she also fit quite well. Chloe had perfect breasts for a woman five foot nine—except that she was only five feet tall. Consequently her breasts were impressive, large and pear-shaped, with just a hint of sag. She also had wide hips and full, beautifully shaped thighs. Her face was heart-shaped, with wide, blue eyes and full, luscious lips. There was more than a hint of plumpness to Chloe, which served her very well in bed. As she had said to Clint the first day they met, "When a man's been to bed with me, he knows he's been to bed."

Clint found that to be an irrefutable truth.

• • •

"So," she said that morning, "have you picked a place yet?"

"No."

"What happens if you don't?" she asked. "Do you lose automatically?"

"No," he said. "I'll pick a place."

"Why haven't you picked something by now?"

"I just can't think of a place where I could go and not meet people who have problems."

"Everyone has problems, Clint," she said sagely. "Just go on ahead and pick a place, and give it your best shot."

"It would have to be someplace where no one knows me," he said, speaking more to himself than to her.

"Try another country, then."

"I've been thinking of that."

He picked up the newspaper from the floor by the bed and started leafing through it.

"I feel like we're married already," Chloe said.

"I'm just trying to stimulate myself somehow."

"I can do that for you," she said, reaching beneath the sheet. "Somehow."

She grabbed him, and he said, "That wasn't the kind of stimulation I had in mind . . . but I'll take it."

As she slid down between his legs and put her talented mouth to work, he dropped the newspaper onto the floor by the bed and reached for her head.

Later, after Chloe had left, he went back to the newspaper. *The Labyrinth Telegraph* was made up mostly of local news, but often they picked up articles from larger newspapers and reprinted them. Clint was hoping to find something that would help him finally make up his mind—and he did.

As soon as he saw the heading of the article he knew it was the answer he was looking for.

He put the newspaper down on the table and pushed it across to Rick.

"Read it," he said.

"The whole paper?"

"Just the article I circled, wise guy," he said, tapping the article in question with the forefinger of his right hand.

Rick picked up the paper and read the headline of the article and then put the paper down.

"I don't have to read any further," he announced, staring at Clint.

The headline of the article read: LONDON GUN EXPO TO BE HELD IN NOVEMBER.

It was the kind of event that had often attracted Clint Adams' attention in the past, but he had never done anything about it before.

Now, because of his bet with Rick Hartman, it seemed the only thing to do.

"You're finally going to go?"

Clint nodded.

"I'm finally going to go."

Clint Adams was going to London, England!

THREE

Clint Adams thought that Piccadilly Circus was a funny name for a street. That was the street that the hotel was located on. He caught a carriage from the docks, and it took him past Buckingham Palace on the way to the hotel. Royalty was not a concept that Clint was very comfortable with. The closest he had ever gotten to meeting royalty was a Russian duke. There was no royalty in the United States—unless you counted the Indians. Some tribes treated their chiefs like royalty, and some even called the chief's daughter a princess.

Clint didn't think he was going to have to worry about meeting any kings or queens here in London. After all, he was only here for a gun expo.

When he arrived at the hotel he was impressed with its size. It almost looked like a castle itself, which was probably why it was called the King's Arms Hotel. The lobby was the largest he had ever seen, even counting some of the bigger hotels in San Francisco and New York.

"Yes, sir?" the desk clerk asked. "May I help you?"

"Yes, I have a reservation."

"Your name, sir?"

11

"Clint Adams."

"Oh, yes, Mr. Adams. You're here for the gun show."

"That's right."

"I'll have a boy carry your bag to your room, sir."

"Thank you."

So far Clint had found everyone he'd met in England to be very polite. It took him a while to understand some of them, but he was catching on to the accent pretty well—unless he ran into one that was especially thick.

He followed the bellboy to his room on the second floor of the four-story hotel.

"I will show you around the room," the boy said. He was actually a man in his forties, who looked ridiculous with the little red pillbox hat on his head.

The room was large, but it *was* only one room, so Clint said, "I can find my way around, thanks," and gave the man two bits.

"Well, if you need anything else, you just ask for Jeffery."

"Jeffery," Clint said. "I'll remember that."

"The restaurant here is the finest in London," Jeffery said, "and so is the pub."

"Pub?"

"Yes," Jeffery said. "Oh, I believe in the States you call them saloons."

"Oh, yeah, saloons. Well, thanks, Jeffery."

"You're welcome, sir."

After the bellboy left Clint sat on the bed and found the mattress firm and comfortable. The furniture in the room looked expensive, and he unpacked his suitcase and put his clothes in the chest of drawers. That done, he took his gun holster out of the bag and set it down on top of the dresser. He hadn't worn it since leaving New York, and on the way to the hotel from the docks he hadn't seen anyone wearing one. He opened the top drawer of the dresser and put the gun inside, then left the room to see if the restaurant was as good as Jeffery said it was.

"What can I get you, sir?" the waitress asked.

She was an extremely pretty girl with black hair and a slim figure.

"Well, I'm not sure, miss," Clint said, studying the menu. "I'm afraid I'm not too familiar with some of the dishes on this menu."

"Are you from America?" she asked, smiling widely.

"Yes, I am."

"How exciting!" she said, her eyes flashing. She had suddenly been transformed from pretty to beautiful. "If you like, I can recommend something."

"I would appreciate it," he said, handing her the menu.

"I'll bring you some steak-and-kidney pie. I think you'll like it."

"Just so long as you bring some strong coffee to go with it."

"Yes, sir."

He watched her walk back to the kitchen to place his order and saw that there were plenty of other men in the dining room who were also watching her.

Some of them were looking at him, too, and he wondered if he was so obviously American—and if so, what was wrong with that?

Clint sat back and thought about his last conversation with Rick Hartman, just before he left Labyrinth . . .

"You want to call off the bet, Clint?"

"Why would I want to do that?"

"Well, you've wanted to make a trip like this for a long time," Rick had said. "I don't feel right about putting this pressure on you."

"Don't worry about the pressure, Rick," Clint had said. "You just worry about what I'm going to ask for when I win this bet."

"There's one thing I don't understand."

"What's that?"

"It says in the article that Samuel Colt is going to be in England. I thought Sam Colt died."

"He did," Clint had said. "That's either a misprint, or somebody's just trying to use Colt's name to draw people. I'll find out when I get there. One thing I do know, there's bound to be *someone* from the Colt company there."

"Are you going to try and sell some of your ideas about modifying guns?"

Clint had grinned and said, "Maybe I'm going to try and learn something."

"You're the best man with a gun I've ever seen," Rick had said, "whether you're shooting it or fixing it. Who's going to teach you anything about guns?"

"The professionals, Rick," Clint had said. "The professionals."

Clint had often wanted to exchange ideas with professionals like the Colts. He was sorry he'd never had a chance to meet Sam Colt. The man had revolutionized the manufacturing of guns, and he had died much too early, in 1861. That made it all the more odd that the newspaper in the U.S. had said he'd be here.

Unless somebody believed in ghosts.

"What was that called?" Clint asked the waitress.

"Steak-and-kidney pie," she said. "How did you like it?"

"It was delicious."

"Would you like some dessert pie now?"

"If you recommend it."

"I do."

She brought him a piece of peach pie and another pot of coffee.

"I appreciate you taking care of me like this," Clint said to her when she brought him his bill. "Without you I might have starved."

"I doubt that very much, sir."

"Clint," he said to her. "My name is Clint Adams."

"Clint."

"And what's your name?"

"Harriet."

"Well, Harriet," he said, "you've already made my trip to England worthwhile."

"Thank you . . . Clint."

Clint stopped at the entrance to the dining room to take one last look at Harriet the waitress, then continued on into the lobby. He wanted to find someone who was connected with the gun exposition.

He wanted to find out about Sam Colt—or his ghost.

FOUR

The gun exposition wasn't due to start for two days yet, but Clint felt sure that someone who was connected with it would be in the hotel somewhere. There were many details to be attended to.

He went to the front desk and asked the same desk clerk who had checked him in if there was anyone he could talk to about the expo.

"Are you connected with it, sir?"

"No, I'm just attending, but I'd like to speak to someone—"

"I could let you speak to our assistant manager, sir, but he really wouldn't know any *particular* details of the event. You would have to speak to the organizers about that."

"I see. Is there someone who is a liaison between the show and the hotel?"

"Yes, sir," the man said. "That would be our Miss Collins."

"Would I be able to speak to Miss Collins?"

"She is not available at the moment, sir, but I could leave her a message. What is your name?"

Clint gave the man his name and his room number, and the man made a note of it.

"Will you be in your room, sir?"

17

"I'm going to walk around outside for a while, but then I'll probably be in my room."

"Yes. A word to the wise, sir, if I may?"

"Go ahead."

"This *is* November in London, sir. It will be very cold and very wet. I would advise you to wear a rather heavy overcoat."

Clint rubbed his jaw and said, "I'm afraid I don't have anything much heavier than this. You see, I was rather ignorant about the weather hereabouts."

"Of course, sir. Well, there are any number of men's stores along Piccadilly Circus where you could buy a coat."

"Does the hotel have a store?"

"It does indeed, sir, but we refrain from recommending our own store. It is not seemly to do so."

Clint knew what he meant. The hotel management did not want it to appear that their employees were simply touting their own store.

"Well, since I'm the one who brought it up," Clint said, "*would* you recommend the hotel store?"

"Indeed I would, sir. It's a fine store."

"How do I get there?"

"Through that hall to your left, sir. There is also an entrance from the outside."

"Thank you."

"You're quite welcome, sir."

When Clint tried to tip the man the clerk waved it away, saying, "That is not at all necessary, sir."

"Thanks again."

Clint left the desk and followed the clerk's directions to the hotel's clothing store to get himself prop-erly outfitted for London in November.

Even with his new coat, the cold worked its way down to his bones, and after walking four blocks he turned and headed back to the hotel. Rather than look-ing at the sights, Clint found himself watching the people. The policemen—or "bobbies," as he had heard them called—all wore blue uniforms with odd-shaped hats, and he especially noticed that the law men did not wear guns. The people strolling Piccadilly appeared to be very well dressed, all wearing stern expressions of a sort. It occurred to Clint that his good friend Bat Masterson would fit in just fine with this Piccadilly atmosphere. He would have to tell Bat about England when he returned to the States.

When he got back to the hotel he decided to go into the dining room for something hot. He caught the clerk's eye to let him know where he'd be, then stopped in the doorway to make sure Harriet was still there, and then made sure he sat at one of her tables.

"Back so soon?" she asked with a smile.

"I made the mistake of going out for a walk."

"Ah, you've discovered winter in London."

"I wonder why I didn't notice it on the way here from the docks."

"You must have passed Buckingham Palace along the way," she said. "Visitors are usually awed by their first sight and tend to forget the cold. Could I bring you some soup to warm you up?"

"Please do."

He was working on the soup when a woman entered the dining room, stopping just inside the door.

She was tall, with thick red hair combed back from her brow, full breasts and hips, and a very businesslike expression on her lovely face. She was wearing a business suit, and he assumed that this was the hotel's Miss Collins.

He waited while she scanned the room, and when her eyes stopped on him he smiled. She frowned, continued looking around, then looked at him again. She was obviously trying to fit him to the description the clerk had given her; she finally decided he must be the one and started toward him. He got to his feet as she reached him.

"Miss Collins?" he asked.

"That's correct," she said. "You are Mr. Adams."

"Yes, Clint Adams. Won't you sit down?"

"For a moment," she said, sitting.

Up close he could see that she had startling green eyes, a patrician nose, and a wide, full-lipped mouth. He would have loved to see that mouth smile, but for the moment its set was very businesslike.

"I understand from George that you are having some difficulty?"

"No, not really," he said. "George—is that the clerk?"

She nodded.

"Well, he must have misunderstood me. I'm just trying to get in touch with one of the organizers of the expo."

"I see. Well, the expo doesn't start for two more days."

"I know that. I wanted to speak to someone before then."

"Well, there are two gentlemen staying at the hotel now, taking care of the final details. A Mister Hyde-White, and Mister Standford."

"Hyde-White?" he asked. "That's one name?"

"Yes," she said. "It's hyphenated."

"I see. Would you be able to leave both gentlemen a message from me? I want to talk to them about Samuel Colt."

"Samuel Colt," she said with a nod, committing the message to memory. "Very well, I will leave them the message."

"Thank you, Miss Collins. By the way. . ."

"Yes?"

"My first name is Clint."

"Yes," she said, standing. "I know. Good day, Mister Adams."

"Good day," he said, standing. By the time he got to his feet she was halfway to the exit.

Harriet came over as he seated himself and said, "I see you've met our Miss Collins."

"Yes, I have."

"Rather a cold fish, she is," Harriet said. "Don't you think?"

He looked up at Harriet and got the impression that she was hoping he *would* think so.

"It appeared so, yes," he said, and she smiled.

"Can I get you some more soup?"

"Yes," he said. "I still seem to be pretty cold."

•   •   •

The man sitting at the corner table kept his eyes on the woman as she talked with the American. He watched her every move very carefully, as he always did. He took great care in picking his victims, which was why there was so much time in between.

Yes, this one would do very nicely. She would definitely be next—if not tonight, then very soon.

Very, very soon.

FIVE

Several hours later, Clint was in his room cleaning his modified Colt when there was a knock on the door. When he opened it there was a white-haired man in his early sixties standing there with a be-mused look on his face.

"Mr. Adams, is it?"

"Yes," Clint said. "It is."

The man extended a pinkish hand and said, "Winston Hyde-White, co-chair of the expo."

"Glad to meet you," Clint said, shaking hands with the man.

"My colleague—Mr. Standford—and I were wondering if you would care to have dinner with us down in the dining room."

"Well, I appreciate the invitation," Clint said, retrieving his hand from the man's surprisingly firm grip. "It's really not necessary, though. I only wanted to ask a question or two—"

"You can ask them over dinner."

"I really don't want to intrude—"

"Nonsense," the man said. "We insist."

"Well . . . in that case, yes, I'd be delighted."

"Good, excellent!" the man said. "A half an hour, then? In the dining room?"

"Yes, half an hour would be fine."

"Excellent!" the man said again. "See you then."

Clint frowned as the man went off down the hall. What had precipitated such an insistent invitation to dinner, he wondered?

Then it hit him.

No.

They couldn't have heard of him.

Not here.

Not all the way over here!

A half an hour later Clint stopped at the entrance to the dining room, spotted Hyde-White and another man seated at a table, and made his way across the floor to them. Hyde-White saw him just as he reached them.

"Mr. Adams," he said, standing up. "Good of you to come, so good." He shook Clint's hand enthusiastically. "This is my colleague, Mr. Edward Standford."

Standford was a barrel-chested individual in his fifties, with flint-gray hair and a bushy mustache. He stood up and shook Clint's hand. In appearance he seemed the more robust of the two, but his handshake was considerably weaker than his colleague's.

"Please sit down and join us," Hyde-White said. "A drink?"

"A beer would be nice."

"Ah!" Standford said. "We'll have the girl bring you a pint of ale. It will put hair on your chest."

Assuming that they were his hosts—they had,

after all, *invited* him to dinner—he said, "Whatever you say, gentlemen."

"Capital!" Standford said.

The waitress turned out to be Harriet, who smiled at Clint and greeted him warmly.

"Bring us three pints, please. There's a good girl," Hyde-White said.

"Certainly, sir."

She gave Clint another warm smile before going off to fetch the drinks.

"When did you arrive?" Hyde-White asked.

"Earlier today."

"Seems your time hasn't been wasted, eh?" Hyde-White asked, eyes twinkling. "That's a lovely young thing."

"A bit thin for my taste," Standford said.

"Edward thinks that because he's so thickly built, his women should be, also," Hyde-White said, laughing. "I think he's afraid he'd crush a thinner woman."

"Winston!"

It seemed that Hyde-White had the sense of humor of the two.

"Tell me, Mr. Adams," Standford said in an attempt to change the subject. "Is it only our little expo that brings you here?"

"Mostly," Clint said. "I was in need of a vacation, and when I saw the announcement I decided to combine the two."

"Well, lucky for us!" Hyde-White said, beaming.

"If you gentlemen don't mind," Clint said, "I'd like to ask a question."

"Of course, of course," Hyde-White said. "Ask away."

"To what do I owe this rather insistent invitation to dinner?" he asked.

The two men exchanged glances, and it was Hyde-White who spoke.

"Why, Mr. Adams, even here—across the pond, as we say—we've heard of your exploits."

"My . . . exploits?" Clint asked with a sinking feeling.

"You *are*, after all, the world-famous Gunsmith, are you not?" Hyde-White asked.

Both men studied him intently, apparently waiting —hoping—for him to confirm their suspicion.

"Um, well, yes, I have been called that," he finally admitted. "I must admit, though, I had no idea that I was . . . *world* famous."

"Well, indeed you are, sir," Hyde-White said. "Imagine our delight when we heard that you were attending our little expo."

"Yes," Clint said. "Imagine."

For the length of the dinner they—actually, Hyde-White did all the talking—asked him about some of his "exploits," as they called them, and Clint was surprised at how much Hyde-White knew about some of his experiences.

"Where did you get all this information?" he finally had to ask.

"Reading," Hyde-White said. "Newspaper articles, mostly."

"And dime novels," Standford added. It was his turn to embarrass his friend.

"All right, yes," the embarrassed Hyde-White admitted. "Dime novels."

Jesus, Clint thought, those things had found their way over here?

Over dessert Clint was finally able to get the subject away from himself.

"May I ask you the questions I wanted to ask?" he asked them both.

"Of course," Standford said. "My partner has, after all, regaled you with stories of your own exploits."

"In the newspaper article I read about the expo, it said that Samuel Colt would be here."

"Yes?" Standford asked.

"Well... to my knowledge Sam Colt died in 1861."

Both men stared at him blankly, and then Standford said suddenly, "Oh, oh, yes, I see your dilemma. We understand that *the* Sam Colt died years ago. The Sam Colt the article was indicating is his son, Samuel *Jarvis* Colt."

"Oh, I see."

"Of course," Hyde-White said, "there is *another* Sam Colt."

SIX

"Yes," Standford said, "Samuel *Caldwell* Colt. He is the original Sam Colt's nephew."

"So it is said," Hyde-White said.

"Winston!"

"What do you mean, so it is said?" Clint asked.

"It's just a rumor," Hyde-White said, as much to his colleague as to Clint. He looked at Clint and said, "There is a rumor that Sam Colt the nephew is actually old Sam Colt's bastard son."

"I see," Clint said.

"It *is* just a rumor," Standford pointed out.

"Well," Clint said, "I certainly won't pass it on any further."

"We would appreciate that," Standford said, glaring at Hyde-White.

"Are there many other American manufacturers who will be attending?"

"The major ones," Standford said. "Winchester, Springfield, and the like."

"I see."

"And the best of our British manufacturers," Hyde-White said.

"And other manufacturers from Europe," Standford said. "Russian, German, French, and others."

"Sounds like more than just a *little* expo."

"It's going to be quite successful," Hyde-White said, smiling happily.

"It could be even more successful," Standford said, "with your help."

Here it comes, Clint thought.

"How?"

Hyde-White picked it up from there. He leaned forward in his chair. "If you would make yourself available to us . . ."

"In what way do you mean 'available'?"

"Well . . . available for people to talk to," Hyde-White said. "Maybe you'd agree to address the expo. You know, tell of some of your exploits—"

"No."

"No?" Standford said.

"I won't talk about myself," Clint said. "If I did, I'd tell the truth."

"And what is wrong with that?" Hyde-White asked.

"The truth I tell won't match what they—or you —have been reading in newspaper articles or in dime novels," he explained.

"Do you mean that all of those stories are . . . fictionalized?" Hyde-White asked.

"Some of them are fiction," Clint said, "and some of them are . . . exaggerated."

"But you are called the Gunsmith in America?" Standford asked.

"Yes."

"And you do have a reputation?"

"Ah, yes . . . but it is not a reputation that I culti-
vate."

"I beg your pardon?" Hyde-White said.

Clint decided to be blunt.

"I don't like it," he said. "I don't like being called
the Gunsmith."

"You don't like the notoriety it brings you?"
Standford asked.

"No, I don't."

"Why?" Hyde-White asked. He was obviously
mystified by Clint's attitude.

"It makes me a target," Clint explained. "It paints
a bull's-eye on my back, on my chest: Every punk
with a gun wants to make a reputation."

Hyde-White and Standford exchanged glances.

"That makes you even more amazing," Hyde-
White finally commented.

"What do you mean?"

"It's even more amazing that you have lasted as
long as you have," Hyde-White said.

"That would make you even more of a draw,"
Standford said.

Suddenly Clint became suspicious of these two
charmers. What if they wanted to publicize the fact
that the Gunsmith was going to be in attendance because their "little" expo was shaping up to be a flop.

"Is this a gun show or a circus?" he asked.

"I'm sorry?" Hyde-White said.

Clint stood up.

"Do you want me to put on a show, too? Shoot a
cigarette out of a woman's mouth?"

"That would be wonderful!" Standford said, thinking Clint was serious.

"I'm afraid not, boys," Clint said. "I didn't come all this way to be exploited."

"Exploited?" Hyde-White said. "Oh, no, no, my dear boy, really—"

"Excuse me, gents," Clint said. "Thanks for the meal."

He turned and walked away from the table quickly—so quickly that he bumped into someone. Dishes and glasses went flying, shattering on the floor. Clint reached out and grabbed ahold of someone to keep them from falling on the breakage.

"My God!" she said.

He looked down and saw that he was holding Harriet in his arms.

"I'm sorry—" he said lamely.

"Don't be," she said, breathing sweetly into his face. "You'll just have to make it up to me—somehow."

In his room Clint thought about what a fool he'd made of himself. First by storming away from the table, and then by slamming into poor Harriet, causing her to drop everything she was carrying. He'd helped her pick everything up and then had gone to his room.

To sulk?

Why should he hold it against Hyde-White and Standford that they'd try to use him to save their expo—if indeed that was their plan. Maybe he'd jumped to conclusions and played the prima donna without cause.

He'd have to decide tonight whether or not he owed them an apology. It wouldn't do to have them angry at him, since he *was* attending their expo. Maybe there was some way he could find out how well their event was going to do without him—and maybe he should be flattered that they thought enough of him to make him the offer.

He wondered idly if they would have offered to pay him, if he'd given them a chance.

There was a knock at his door then. He wondered if one or both of the partners had come up to apologize to *him*.

When he opened it, it wasn't Hyde-White or Standford, it was the waitress, Harriet.

She smiled at him and said, "I told you you'd have to make it up to me, love."

SEVEN

"Come in," he said, stepping back.

Harriet entered the room, and he gently closed the door behind her. She had changed from her work clothes to a simple black dress that showed off her figure. Her breasts were small, but they were firm. She was tall, and most of her height was her long legs.

"You didn't get fired, did you?" he asked.

She turned to face him.

"No, love, I didn't get fired," she said. "I've broken dishes before. No, I told the boss you stepped on my foot and that I wanted to get off of it."

"Your foot is all right, isn't it?"

"Oh, it's fine," she said, moving closer to him. "But I do want to get off my . . . feet."

She put her arms around his neck and kissed him, gently at first, and then more insistently until her tongue pushed past his lips. He slid his arms around her slim waist and pulled her to him.

"Mmm," she said against his mouth. "You *are* strong. I noticed that when you knocked me down."

"I didn't knock you down."

She pulled his shirt out of his pants and said, "Well, you almost did." Running her hands beneath

35

his shirt and over his chest she said, "Now you have a second chance."

He took hold of her by the upper arms, backed her up to his bed, and pushed her down onto it. She moved to a seated position and started to shuck her clothes. He had already removed his boots when he first came to his room, so now he discarded his shirt and pants and sundries and joined her on the bed . . .

The first time they were both eager, groping and grabbing, tasting and touching . . .

The next time was slower, easier. He kissed her breasts and ran his fingers between her legs, wetting her. She moaned as his mouth traveled down over her belly and cried out when his tongue tasted her. He kept flicking his tongue over her and reached up to manipulate her nipples at the same time.

She moaned and writhed, digging her firm butt into the mattress, turning her face into the pillow so she could cry out louder when she came.

He straddled her then, sliding himself into her slowly, inch by inch. She reached for him blindly, tossing her head from side to side. When he was firmly inside of her he slid his hands beneath her to cup her firm buttocks and moved inside of her in long, slow strokes.

"Oh, yes, love, yes, like that . . ." she moaned. "Slowly, ever so slowly . . ."

She moved her hips in unison with his and raked his back with her nails until they both came together so violently that they moved the bed . . . and maybe even the earth.

Definitely the bed.

Down in her office Lesley Anne Collins was working late. That is, she was *trying* to work. It was annoying to her that she couldn't stop thinking about a man she had met only that same day—and an American at that.

She had known many men in her life, but never had she been immediately attracted to one. She had always taken her time getting to know a man before deciding that, yes, he was worthy of her.

Lesley Anne Collins knew she was a snob. In fact, she worked hard at it. She had a naturally high opinion of herself, and a naturally low opinion of the rest of mankind. It was ingrown. It happened when you grew up wealthy and then became wealthier through no fault of your own. This job was actually an attempt on her part to change her attitude.

It wasn't working.

And now this, an ignominious attraction to a man she didn't know, and whom she could not stop thinking about.

She'd just have to go home and try harder.

"I have to go," Harriet said.

"You can't."

"I have the breakfast shift tomorrow."

"I'm sorry," Clint said, "but you can't go."

"Why not?" Harriet asked, smiling.

"You haven't told me your last name."

"Oh . . . well, it's Carlyle, Harriet Carlyle."

"Can I see you home, Harriet Carlyle?"

"No," she said, putting her hand against his chest. "That won't be necessary. I'll see you tomorrow—if you want to see me, that is."

"Oh," he said, rubbing her arm. "I think I could be persuaded."

He watched with pleasure as she dressed, and then she leaned down to kiss him before leaving.

"I'll buy you breakfast in the morning," she said and left.

He wondered idly if she could be fired for that.

EIGHT

The man was waiting across the street from the hotel, waiting for the woman to leave. This was the night, dear lady.

The woman left the hotel by the front door, pulling the folds of her coat tightly around her to repel the cold. You would think that having been born in London, she'd be used to it by now.

She started off down Piccadilly, her strides long and confident, her carriage proud and erect. She had no idea what was waiting for her just a half a block away.

The man waited in an alley. This late in the evening even Piccadilly was quiet, and he could hear her footsteps on the concrete walk. The steps came closer and closer and then she was . . . there!

He reached out and caught hold of the back of her collar, using it to pull her into the alley. She tried to scream, but he was too quick for her. His other arm snaked beneath her chin and pressed tightly against her throat, cutting off her cry.

He dragged her further into the darkness of the alley and pushed her down on the ground. He moved his arm and pressed one hand to her throat, holding her down that way while he reached into his pocket with the other. He brought a silk scarf out of his pocket, wrapped it around her throat, and then squeezed. Before long she was dangling from the scarf, the life choked out of her.

He looked down at the dead woman, holding her head just off the ground with the scarf, then he released one end of the scarf so that it came free from her neck, dropping her so that the back of her head hit the hard ground.

He placed the scarf on her chest, then realized that the wind would probably blow it away, so he wrapped it around her neck again, left it there, and took his leave of the alley.

He would now have to decide what color scarf to use next time.

NINE

The knocking on the door was insistent, jarring Clint awake.

"Hold on, hold on," he said, staggering from the bed. His foot got caught on the blanket, and he stumbled across the room and slammed into the door with his shoulder.

"Jesus Christ!" he shouted out in pain. He yanked the door open and shouted, "This had better be good!"

The man at the door smiled tightly, showed Clint a badge, and said, "I think we can make it interesting enough for you."

Clint Adams' first visit to Scotland Yard was not a pleasant one.

"Tell us again, Mr. Adams."

"Tell you what?"

"How you met the dead woman," the chief inspector said. "And of your liaison with her."

"I've told you already."

"Tell us again," the inspector said. "Please."

The chief inspector was the man who had come to Clint's room that morning to bring him to Scotland Yard. His name was James Reed, and he was a tall,

41

elegant-looking man in his early forties, who thought that the strangulation murder of a young waitress was enough to bring him out from behind his desk and involve him actively in the investigation.

"I met her when she waited on me in the hotel dining room," Clint explained for the fifth time. "Our liaison, as you put it, was instigated by her. She came to my room."

"And you let her in?"

"Yes."

"Are you in the habit of . . . sleeping with strange women, Mr. Adams?" the inspector asked. "Or women of such short acquaintance?"

The inspector was just too smug for Clint, so he said, "As a matter of fact, Inspector, I am."

"Why is that, sir?"

"I like women."

"And they like you?"

"They seem to."

The inspector sneered at Clint and said, "We have a name for men like you in this country, Mr. Adams."

"That's funny," Clint said. "We have a name for men like you in my country, Inspector. Shall we swap?"

The inspector moved towards Clint's chair so quickly that Clint thought the man was going to strike him. He might have, too, if the door hadn't opened at that moment.

"Inspector?" a young man said.

"What is it?" Reed shouted.

"I have the information you requested on Mr.

Adams," the man said. He was holding a sheaf of papers in his hands. They looked like telegraph flimsies.

The inspector glared at Clint for a moment and then turned and took the papers from the man.

"That's all," he said, and the man nodded and left.

Reed took a moment to scan the papers, then put them aside on a table.

"I see you have a reputation."

"Is that so?"

"You were a law enforcement officer once."

"A long time ago."

"And now you live by your gun."

Clint didn't comment on that.

"A common gunman."

That rankled Clint.

"If you have enough information on me, Inspector, you know that I'm not *so* common."

"No, that is true enough," Reed said. "Why are you here in London, Mr. Adams?"

"I'm surprised you haven't asked me that before," Clint commented.

"Just answer the question!" Reed said sharply.

"I'm here for a gun exposition that's being held at the hotel."

"And that's all?"

"Yes, that's all," Clint said. "I did not come here to murder a young woman I hardly knew."

"I see," the inspector said. "You knew her well enough to have a carnal liaison with her, but not well enough to kill her. Is that it?"

"Carnal liaison?" Clint repeated. "Come on, Inspector. Loosen up a bit here."

Clint had a feeling he was paying for the fact that Inspector Reed was a prude.

"Look, mister—" Reed said tightly, but he was once again interrupted, this time by a knock on the door.

"Yes?" he shouted.

The door opened, and the same young man stuck his head in, obviously expecting it to be chopped off.

"Uh, Inspector, there are a couple of gentlemen out here who would like to talk to you."

"About what?"

"Uh, about him, sir," the man said, inclining his head towards Clint.

The inspector threw Clint an ugly look and then told the younger man, "Stay with him!"

"Yessir."

After the inspector left, Clint decided to talk to the other man.

"He's a hard man, the inspector."

The man grinned and said, "The hardest . . . but he's fair."

"A bit of a prude, isn't he?"

The man suddenly looked as if he were afraid someone might be listening to them.

"I hadn't noticed that," he said, and from then on he stopped talking.

After about fifteen minutes the inspector entered the room again, looking no happier than when he left.

"I've just talked to two gentlemen named Hyde-White and Standford," he said to Clint.

"So?"

"They tell me that you are part of their expo. Is that true?"

Clint decided to play along.

"It is."

"Why didn't you tell me that?"

"To tell the truth, Inspector," Clint said, "you never gave me the chance. Besides, would it have made such a difference?"

Reed didn't answer.

"Look, Adams, the girl was seen going into your room, so there's every reason to believe that you were the last person to see her alive."

"Except for the desk clerk, who saw her leave," Clint pointed out.

"Yes, well—"

"And the doorman, who *let* her out."

"The doorman did—"

"Then why are you coming down on *me*, Inspector?" Clint demanded. "Is it because the clerk or the doorman hadn't *slept* with her?—that you know of, of course."

The inspector's jaw tightened, and he said, "Get out of here. Don't even think about leaving London until I say so."

Clint took his jacket from the back of his chair and stood up.

"I'd like my gun."

Reed laughed.

"I'd like to be a millionaire," he said. "Neither is liable to happen today. Get out."

Clint decided to let it go—for now.

As he started past the inspector, Reed grabbed him by the arm.

"If you killed that girl, mate, I'll have you."

"I tell you what, *mate*," Clint said. "Maybe I'll just put that killer in your damn lap. Then you can apologize to me right in the middle of Piccadilly Circus."

Clint jerked his arm free and left the room.

TEN

When he left Scotland Yard Clint found both Hyde-White and Standford waiting for him with a carriage.

"May we offer you a ride, sir?" Hyde-White asked.

"Why not?" he said. "It's the two of you who got me out of there—with a lie, I might add."

"Did you support that lie?" Standford asked.

"I did."

"Then it's not a lie anymore, is it?"

Clint climbed aboard and said, "No, I don't suppose it is."

"Had breakfast yet?" Hyde-White asked.

"No."

"Then we might as well talk over breakfast," the older man said and signaled his driver to drive on.

When Clint entered the dining room he found himself expecting to see Harriet waiting to serve him. He was disappointed when she wasn't. It would have meant that the morning had either been a dream, or somebody was lying.

There was no dream.

No lie.

Harriet Carlyle was dead.

He sat at a table with the two men who were running the expo, and he ordered coffee.

"No breakfast?" Hyde-White asked.

"Can't say I'm very hungry right now, Mr. Hyde-White," he replied.

"Well, I hope you won't mind if we eat."

"Go right ahead."

The two men placed their orders, and the waiter went off to get them.

"It seems I'm in your debt, gentlemen," Clint said. "Can't say I don't know what it is you want from me in return."

"Now, Mr. Adams—may I call you Clint?" Hyde-White asked.

"Sure."

"We don't want to force you into anything."

"That's why you put me in a position where I had to tell the police I was working for your expo?"

"That was the fastest way to get you out," Standford said. "The inspector knows both of us, and he knows how much this expo means to us."

"Let's put our cards on the table, shall we, gents?" Clint said.

"By all means," Standford said.

"Just how successful do you expect this expo to be—uh, without me, that is?"

The two men exchanged glances, and then Standford spoke. He was obviously the businessman of the two.

"We expected it to do quite well," Standford said, "but our registration isn't what we hoped."

"Why?"

"We don't know."

"And you think I can save it? The expo starts tomorrow, doesn't it?"

"And will go on for five days," Standford said. "If you agree to be part of it—today—we can get the word out fast enough to do us some good."

"What if people don't know who I am, the way you two fellas do?"

"Then we'll tell them," Standford said.

Suddenly Clint revised his opinion of the two men sitting with him. He had originally thought they were businessmen.

Now he knew he was sitting with a couple of promoters. He'd known a lot of promoters in his time—Bat Masterson was one of the best—and he wondered how good these two were.

He was curious enough to find out.

"All right, gentlemen," Clint said. "Since I'm here, I'll be part of your little expo."

"Capital!" Hyde-White said happily.

"On one condition."

"What's that?" Standford asked.

"I don't intend to be paraded around like a trained bear," Clint said, "and I won't make any speeches. I'll talk to people—about guns, and that's all."

Standford looked at Hyde-White and then said, "All right. Agreed."

"And I want to meet the Colt people."

"Don't worry, Clint," Hyde-White said, rubbing his hands together happily. "You'll be meeting everyone."

ELEVEN

After breakfast they ordered a second pot of coffee, and both Hyde-White and Standford lit up cigars. Clint declined when they offered him one. He liked the way cigar smoke smelled, but he didn't like the way the damned things tasted.

"Tell me something," he said.

"What?" Hyde-White asked.

"You said the inspector knew you," Clint said. "Does that mean you know him?"

"I knew his father," Hyde-White said. "I've known James since he was a tad."

"Tell me about him."

"What would you want to know?"

"Well, he was pretty hard on me because the dead girl had been seen coming from my room."

"Is that so?" Standford said, looking at Clint with interest.

"That's not hard to understand, Clint," Hyde-White said.

"Why not?"

"James had a wife, a beautiful wife. They were married ten years. About three years ago they . . . divorced."

"Why?"

"Well, he found out that she was cheating on him."

"With who?"

Hyde-White rubbed his jaw and said, "Well . . . everybody."

"What do you mean, everybody?"

"Just what I said," Hyde-White said. "He found out that since the first day they were married she'd been sleeping around with anything in pants. Salesmen, milk men, his *friends*—fact is, she slept with his best man an hour after the wedding."

"How do you know that?"

"I saw them together."

"And you didn't tell him?"

"What could I say to a man who had just gotten married? No, I'd hoped Lisa would . . . change after some time."

"And she never did?"

"She got worse," he said, a look of distaste on his face. "She was no better than a whore, except she never charged money. She gave it away to anyone who would take it."

"And that's why he's so . . . prudish?"

"He has no friends left, and little regard for a man or woman who sleeps around."

"Well," Clint said, "I can't say I really blame him for that. I can understand why he was so hard on me."

"Don't judge him too harshly, Clint," Hyde-White said. "He's a good man, a good policeman."

"The dead girl," Clint said. "Will she get a fair shake from him?"

"Oh, yes," Hyde-White said with certainty. "As I said, he's a good policeman. It wouldn't matter if she *was* a whore. He'd find out who killed her."

"Well, that's good," Clint said. "She was a real nice girl."

"Wait a minute," Hyde-White said. "Is the dead girl the same girl who served us here last night?"

"She is," Clint said, then added, "was. If you gentlemen don't mind, I was rousted pretty early this morning. I'd like to get cleaned up."

"Of course, of course," Hyde-White said. "We understand."

"You'll let me know what you want me to do?"

"We will be in touch," Standford said.

Clint stood up, started to leave, and then stopped.

"Oh, about the way I acted last night—"

"Think nothing of it," Hyde-White said.

"Perhaps we went about things the wrong way, Clint," Standford said. "Why don't we just start fresh?"

"All right," Clint agreed. "I'd like that. I'll talk to you later."

As Clint Adams disappeared into the lobby, Hyde-White said to Standford, "Drink up, old chap. We've got some promoting to do."

Chief Inspector James Reed sat at his desk, holding a silk scarf in his hands. It was purple, and it was strong. He knew that because he wrapped it around his hands and pulled on it until his blood circulation was cut off. It certainly made an effective weapon with which to strangle someone.

He thought back to a time when he had thought about killing someone just the way that girl had been killed last night.

There was a time when he thought he wanted to kill his wife—his ex-wife—Lisa. She'd made a fool of him and made him waste ten years of his life. For that he could have killed her easily, but he was a policeman. If he *had* killed her he would have lost that, and being a policeman was the one thing that had kept him sane since the divorce.

He smoothed the scarf out now on his desk and studied it as if he were waiting for it to tell him something. Then he turned it over, and it did.

On the other side, tight against the stitched seam, was a small label. It said: THE KING'S ARMS HOTEL.

That was the hotel where the girl had worked.

It was also the hotel where Clint Adams was staying.

TWELVE

Clint went back to his room with the intention of catching up on some of the sleep he'd been denied when the police had rousted him that morning. As it turned out, he couldn't sleep. He was bothered by Harriet Carlyle's murder. Who could she have offended so much that they would drag her into a dark alley and kill her that way?

He was lying on his bed with his hands behind his back, staring at the ceiling, when someone knocked on the door. The first thing Clint thought about was his gun, which was over at Scotland Yard.

He got up and opened the door.

"Not again," he said as he eyed Chief Inspector James Reed. "Are you going to drag me back down to Scotland Yard, Inspector?"

"No," Reed said. "What I have to say can be said here."

"Well, come in, then."

The inspector took one tentative step, then looked past Clint at the bed and stopped.

"Inspector?"

"I'll talk from here," Inspector Reed said, taking a step back.

"All right, then, talk."

"You did some shopping in the hotel store yesterday, didn't you?"

"I did."

"What did you buy?"

"A coat."

"That's all?"

"That's all, Inspector," Clint said, frowning. "What else am I supposed to have bought?"

"Maybe a scarf?" Reed said, taking one out of his pocket. "A purple silk scarf, like this one."

Clint eyed the scarf.

"Is that the one . . .?"

"This is the one that killed the girl."

"Harriet," Clint said. "She had a name; it was Harriet Carlyle."

"I know her name."

"Well, then use it when you talk about her!" Clint said. He turned his back and walked into the room.

"I'm not finished—"

"If you've got more to say to me you can damn well come inside and say it."

He didn't bother to turn and see if the man had entered the room. Suddenly he wanted a drink, but it was too damned early.

"Did the girl—did Harriet Carlyle say anything to you about someone bothering her lately, maybe following her?" Reed asked.

"No," Clint said. "No." And then, perversely, "We didn't talk much."

"This scarf was bought in the hotel store, Adams."

"That doesn't mean I bought it," Clint said.

"There are a lot of guests in this hotel, and people can walk in off the street and buy things." He turned and said, "Besides, if you've talked to the clerk in the store you know I only bought a coat."

"I talked to him."

"Then why are you bothering me?"

"Because you're my number one suspect."

"You know I didn't buy the damn thing!"

"I don't know that you didn't steal it," Reed said, putting the scarf into his pocket.

"Well," Clint said, "you got anything else to ask me?"

"No."

"Then, good day."

Reed hesitated, then turned to leave.

"Inspector."

"Yes?" Reed said, turning back.

"You had better find the killer before I do," Clint said. "It might be hard to understand, but I liked that girl."

Reed stared at Clint for a few moments and then said, "No, it's not hard to understand at all, Mr. Adams."

The inspector left, and Clint closed the door behind him. For some reason he thought that perhaps he had made some points with the inspector.

He wished he knew how.

He decided to go downstairs and get that drink he wanted. It may have been early to drink, but it was too damn early for Harriet Carlyle to die, too.

• • •

Inspector James Reed stopped in the lobby and thought about Clint Adams. The man didn't strike him as a killer—not that kind of a killer, anyway. Oh, he knew about his 'Gunsmith' reputation, but he was sure many of those had been other men who had been trying to kill him.

He wondered about the man's vehement attitude toward the dead girl, toward Harriet Carlyle. Could he have cared for that girl so much after only one day?

What kind of man was he, anyway, beyond the reputation with a gun?

Reed fingered the scarf in his pocket and thought that perhaps he'd attend this gun expo, after all. He'd known about it, but certainly had had no intention of attending it. He didn't like guns very much.

He often thought that if he'd had a gun at the moment he'd found out about Lisa, he probably would have killed her. That was why he didn't like them.

They were too damn easy to kill with.

THIRTEEN

Clint found the hotel saloon—or "pub," as Jeffery the bellboy had called it—and ordered himself a whiskey. It was after noon, so the bartender gave it to him without question.

When the man brought it Clint said, "Did you know Harriet Carlyle?"

"Harriet?" the man said. "The girl who was killed?"

"That's right."

"I knew her."

The bartender was a big man with huge hands, gnarly knuckles, sloping shoulders, and a battered face. He appeared to be in his forties and had been at one time, Clint would have bet, a fighter.

"Was she involved with anyone?"

"What do you mean, 'involved'?"

"I mean, was she keeping company with anyone?"

"Why do you want to know?"

"Because somebody killed her," Clint said. "I liked her, and I'd like to try and find out who."

"Isn't that a job for Scotland Yard?"

"Has anyone from Scotland Yard talked to you yet?"

"Sure. Chief Inspector Reed."

"And what did you tell him?"

"Well, I told him that I didn't know Harriet that well. She kept to herself, pretty much."

"So why can't you tell me that?"

The man scratched his head and said, "Well, I guess I have."

"That's right," Clint said, "you have." Clint paid for the whiskey and said, "Thanks for the drink."

When he got to the desk, the same man who had checked him in was there.

"Were you working last night when Harriet left the hotel?"

"No, I wasn't," the man said. "Our night man was working."

"What time does he come to work?"

"At six P.M., sir."

"Thank you. Oh, what about the doorman?"

"The same thing, sir. The night doorman will come on at six."

"All right, thank you."

Clint questioned the dining room and kitchen staff next. He found one waitress who considered herself a friend of Harriet's. Her name was Annie Potts, and she was about Harriet's age, only not as pretty.

"Was she keeping company with anyone, Annie?"

Annie shrugged. "She had boyfriends on and off, but nobody special."

"How long did she stay with one boyfriend?"

"Not very long."

"Could one of them have gotten angry enough after she left him to kill her?"

"I don't know, mister. You know, I answered all these questions for the inspector from Scotland Yard."

"Yes," he said. "I know. Thanks for answering them for me."

He went to see the clerk in the store next.

"Do you remember who you sold that scarf to?"

"I told the inspector that I did not."

"It's a rather expensive item, isn't it?"

"That it is."

"Then how many could you sell?"

"You would be surprised, sir," the clerk said. "We have many customers who would be able to afford an item like that."

"Yes, I suppose you do," he said. "All right, thank you."

"I told the inspector you didn't buy a scarf," the man called after him.

"I appreciate it," Clint said. "Thanks."

Clint got to the door that led to the lobby and then turned.

"You don't sell guns here, do you?"

"No, sir, we do not."

Clint nodded, waved, and went into the lobby.

The man sitting in the lobby saw Clint Adams come out of the hotel store. He knew that Scotland Yard had questioned him about the murder. He wondered what he had been doing in the store, since he

walked out empty-handed. Asking questions, probably, just as the inspector had been doing earlier.

It was a good thing he had bought all the scarves
he needed already.

He wondered idly if the clerk in the store would
remember the man who had bought five scarves last
month.

It wouldn't do if he suddenly did.

It wouldn't do at all.

FOURTEEN

After spending the day asking questions, Clint decided that he'd wasted his time dogging the inspector's tracks. He was also somewhat gratified that he had asked all the same questions that a trained Scotland Yard inspector had asked. Still, he didn't know much more about Harriet Carlyle's death than he had before.

Because it would remind him of Harriet, he decided not to have dinner that night in the hotel. He spotted Jeffery in the lobby and called him over.

"Yes, sir? What can I do for you?"

"If I wanted a meal—a good meal—outside of the hotel, where would I go?"

"Why would you want to eat outside the hotel?" Jeffery asked. "The food is excellent, and it's very cold out."

"Just answer my question, Jeffery."

"All right, sir," Jeffery said. "There's a restaurant a few blocks down that isn't bad. They make a pretty good steak-and-kidney pie."

Steak-and-kidney pie. He didn't care if he never had steak-and-kidney pie again.

"Could I just get steak and potatoes there?"

"Yes, sir, I imagine you could."

"All right, give me directions."

"Simple enough," the bellboy said. "Just out the front door, turn left, and walk three blocks."

"Fine," Clint said. "Thanks."

"Is there anything I could help you with, sir?"

Clint thought a moment, then said, "Yes. Where is the nearest gun shop?"

"Aren't too many gun shops to be found," Jeffery said. "Even the bobbies don't carry guns."

"Let me put it this way," Clint said. "Could you get me a gun if I wanted one?"

Jeffery smiled, revealing a gap in his smile where an eyetooth used to be.

"I can get you whatever you want, Mr. Adams— for the right price."

"I'll keep that in mind, Jeffery."

"Enjoy your meal."

Clint nodded and went out into the cold. By the time he returned, both the night desk clerk and the night doorman should be on duty.

The clerk in the hotel store locked the doors and prepared to go home for the night. First he locked the door that led to the lobby, and then on his way out he locked behind him the door that led to the street.

When he started for home he took the opposite direction that Harriet Carlyle had taken the night before.

That didn't save him.

The man dragged the body of the clerk through the alley to the other side, where he had a carriage waiting behind the hotel. He dumped the body inside, climbed up, and started off. He was going to have to dump the body somewhere where it wouldn't be found. He didn't want people to find out the clerk was dead until he was finished. Also, he'd had to kill him with a knife, because he didn't have a scarf to waste.

Besides, the scarves were for the women.

All five of them.

The food at the restaurant may not have been as good as the food in the hotel, but it was good enough for Clint. He was also careful to seat himself where he'd be waited on by a waiter, not a waitress. He didn't want any waitresses showing up at his door for a while.

Not for a long while.

When Clint returned to the hotel he saw there was a different doorman at the door.

As the man opened the door for him he said, "You saw Harriet leave the hotel last night?"

"Harriet?" the man said, frowning. "Oh, you mean the waitress who was killed?"

"Yes."

"Yes, I saw her."

"Did anyone leave the hotel after her?"

"I saw no one leave after her, sir."

"Did you see anyone follow her?"

"I did not."

Clint sighed and said, "All right, thank you."

As he went into the hotel the doorman said, "I

told all that to the inspector from Scotland Yard."

"Yes," Clint said. "I know you did."

He went through the same thing with the night desk clerk and got the same answers.

No one had seen anything.

He decided to go to bed. The next day the expo would start, and he was sure that Hyde-White and Standford would have plenty for him to do. Leave it to Reed and the rest of Scotland Yard to find the man who had killed Harriet. That was their job.

He *was* supposed to be here on vacation.

FIFTEEN

There was no pounding on the door the next morning, for which Clint was very grateful. He washed and dressed for the expo, putting on the one suit he had brought with him. Putting it on he had the uncomfortable feeling that he was going to have to buy a new suit. If he did, maybe he'd let Hyde-White and Standford pay for it. After all, he was *their* trained bear.

Out of reflex he reached for his gun before he realized it wasn't there. He wished now that he had thought to bring another, maybe the little Colt New Line, but he hadn't imagined he'd really need a gun —not here, not while on vacation, where no one knew who he was.

Sure.

Clint went down to the lobby, wondering why he hadn't heard from the partners as to what they wanted him to do. When he got there he stopped short and stared. There was a poster in the lobby announcing to all the world that the famous GUN-SMITH, THE LEGEND OF THE AMERICAN WEST, was attending the expo.

Clint was still staring at it when Lesley Anne Collins came up alongside him, her arms folded beneath

67

her breasts. Together they stared at it for a little longer.

"Tacky, isn't it?" she finally said.

He looked at her and said, "Uh, it is a little lurid. I mean, the print is so . . . *red*!"

"Yes, it is," she said. "I am starting to be very sorry that we allowed this expo to be presented here."

"Who made that decision?"

"My boss."

He turned to face her now and said, "My first name is still Clint, Miss Collins."

She looked at him, then smiled.

"Yes, well, I'm sorry about that, Mr. Adams," she said. "My name is Lesley Anne."

"I'm very pleased to meet you."

"And I'm pleased to meet you," she said and then cast another glance at the poster and said, "I think."

"You have to believe me when I say I had nothing to do with this."

"Oh, I do," she said. She tilted her head to one side to study the poster again and asked, "Are you really a legend of the American West?"

"Uh, some people have said so," he said, feeling somewhat embarrassed.

"You don't think so?"

"I try not to think of it at all."

"Then why this?" she asked, indicating the poster.

"As I said, I have nothing to do with this."

"But you are attending the expo."

"Yes."

"And I assume you have given them permission to publicize the fact."

"Well . . . yes."

"Why? Why allow them to exploit you this way?"

"It's a long story, Miss Collins," he said. "Maybe you'd let me tell it to you over lunch later today?"

Now she looked at him and studied him, cocking her head to one side as she had done with the poster.

"Maybe I will," she said. "Come and see me at my office at one."

"I will," he said, then added, "as long as these two don't have me jumping through hoops."

"Somehow," she said, moving away from him, "I doubt that."

Clint turned away from the lurid poster to watch her walk away and wondered what had caused her sudden change in attitude. Maybe the first time they had met she was just having a bad day.

When she moved out of sight down a hallway he assumed led to her office, he turned again and looked for Hyde-White and Standford. His eyes fell on the front door of the hotel store, and he noticed that it was closed. If he remembered correctly it opened very early—usually.

He went to the desk and said, "Pardon me."

"Yes, sir?"

"What time does the store open?"

The man suddenly looked annoyed. "I am sorry, sir," he said. "Normally it is open by now, but the man who runs it did not come to work today. We are presently finding someone who will open. I'm sure it will be open soon."

"Thank you."

"Again, I apologize if you have been caused any inconvenience by this—"

Clint silenced him by waving his hand and saying, "No, no, it's all right. There's no inconvenience. Can you tell me where the expo is set up?"

"Of course, sir. Through those double doors and downstairs, in the King's Hall."

"The King's Hall," Clint said. "Thank you."

Clint went through the double doors and downstairs. There were a couple of hallways, but there was also a sign telling him that the King's Hall was to the right. When he reached it the door was closed and locked, but he could hear activity behind it, and he saw some shadows beneath the door. He knocked on the door, and when there was no answer, he pounded on it.

Finally someone opened it: a tall man in a work shirt, looking less than thrilled.

"Yes, what is it?"

"I'm looking for either Mr. Hyde-White or Mr. Standford."

"Well, I haven't got any bloody idea where they are, mate!" the man said. "Can I get back to work now? We've got to put this act on the road in less than half an hour, you know."

"I'm sorry," Clint said. He tried to get a peek inside, but the man pulled the door closed too quickly for him.

Clint decided to go and have breakfast and let the partners find *him*.

He was on his way up the stairs when the double

doors opened and Chief Inspector James Reed stepped through and started down. They both stopped halfway and stared at each other.

"Where are you going?" Reed asked.

"To breakfast," Clint said. "Would you like to join me?"

Reed shrugged and said, "Why not?" and they both went back upstairs.

SIXTEEN

The inspector ordered something called kippers, which Clint decided not to ask about. He ordered as American a breakfast as he could get: eggs and bacon and some biscuits. They both started on coffee while they waited for the food to come.

"What were you looking for when you came down those stairs?" Clint asked.

"You."

"Should I be flattered or worried?"

"How about truthful?"

"I have been up until now."

"You have been walking in my shadow."

Clint frowned a moment, then realized what the inspector meant.

"If you mean I've been dogging your trail, I guess you're right."

"Why?"

"I told you," Clint said. "I want to find out who killed Harriet Carlyle."

"So do I."

"Then there's no reason for us to be so wary around one another."

"Well, there is one reason."

"I'm still a suspect."

"That's right."

"What can I do to clear myself?"

"Well, for one thing, you can arrange to be somewhere else when the next girl is killed."

"The next girl?" Clint asked. "You mean you expect there to be another one?"

"I am afraid there will be."

"Why?"

"The scarf."

"What about it?"

The inspector used the thumb and forefinger of his right hand to wipe each side of his mouth, then did it again. Clint suspected it was a habitual gesture.

"I don't know exactly why I am telling you this."

"You either want me to help," Clint said, "or you're trying to trap me."

"I don't think I'm that clever."

"Oh," Clint said, "I think you are. What is it you want to tell me?"

"The scarf," the inspector said again. "It's been used before. Oh, not the same scarf, but—"

"I understand what you mean," Clint assured him. "Where has it been used before?"

"France, three years ago," Reed said. "Five women were killed."

"Did they catch the killer?"

"No," Reed said. "The murders stopped after five, and the killer just disappeared."

"And you think this might be the same killer?"

"It could be."

"Well, then, I'm in the clear," Clint said. "I've never even been to France."

"There's another theory."

"Which is?"

"This killer may simply be copying the method of the French killer."

"This killer would have to know about the French killer," Clint said. "Which means he was either in France at the time or he's read about it."

"It *has* been written up in some law enforcement journals, and I believe it has been publicized in the United States."

"Which means I remain a suspect."

"Yes."

"Just between you and me?"

"Yes?"

"Do you think I did it?"

Again, the habitual gesture, thumb and forefinger rubbing the corners of his mouth.

"No."

"Why not?"

"Your reaction to the girl—to Harriet Carlyle's murder. I don't quite understand it, but it is not the reaction of a man who killed her."

"What don't you understand?"

"Why you would react so vehemently to the murder of a girl you hardly knew."

"I slept with her."

"I . . . know."

"Despite what I might have said to you before, we did talk some. I liked her. I don't like seeing people I like get killed."

"It has happened before?"

"I've lived around violence most of my adult life, Inspector. Sometimes I think it follows me around."

"Are you saying you feel responsible for Harriet Carlyle's death?"

"No, I'm not saying that," Clint said. "I'm just saying the violence doesn't surprise me. It makes me angry, but it doesn't surprise me. Not anymore. Not for a long, long time."

The breakfast came, and as they sat back to allow the waiter to serve them, Clint caught Reed's eye and said, "Helluva way to live, huh?"

SEVENTEEN

From there the conversation became more personal. Clint told the inspector that he was born in the eastern United States but had gone west as a very young man. He drifted into law enforcement, became fascinated with guns, started taking them apart, putting them back together again, and found out he could hit what he wanted to hit anytime he wanted to, by just pointing.

"Have you killed many men with a gun?"

"Some."

"I despise guns."

"Why?"

"It is too easy to kill with one," Reed said. "If men could only kill each other with their bare hands, I don't think they would enjoy it so much."

"You think men enjoy killing each other?"

"They do it too often not to," Reed said. He realized what he might be implying and said, "I hope you understand I'm not talking about you specifically."

"No offense taken, Inspector, but you can't blame the gun for what the man—or woman—does with it."

"Nevertheless," Reed insisted, "the simple existence of guns has increased the number of deaths a hundredfold over the course of the years."

Clint decided that he and the inspector could argue the pros and cons of guns into infinity. Most likely the question of guns, good or bad, would go on being argued until then anyway, by many others. Why should they start now?

To Clint's surprise, the inspector talked about his past, his early days as a policeman, and then shocked Clint by talking about his wife.

"I could have killed her," he said. Clint looked at the inspector's hands and saw that they were trembling. "If I'd had a gun, I think I would have."

"Have you ever killed anyone?"

Reed looked directly into Clint's eyes.

"In all my years as a policeman, no, I have never had to kill anyone. Do you find that odd?"

"On the contrary," Clint said. "I find it very commendable."

"Do you wish you had never killed your first man?" Reed asked.

Clint smiled ruefully and said, "I wish I had never killed anyone, Inspector, but wishing is for children. Adults have to live in the real world . . . don't we?"

Reed nodded and said, "All too often."

When they finished breakfast Clint asked the inspector if he would have more coffee, but Reed declined.

"I have to get back to work."

"Any other suspects?"

Reed stood up and said, "We're rounding up the

usual habitual villains, but there are no specific suspects."

"Except me."

Reed stared at Clint, then said, "Technically speaking, yes."

Clint nodded his understanding.

"By the way," Reed said.

"Yes?"

"In 'dogging my tracks,' as you put it, have you learned anything interesting?"

"Everyone I spoke to told me the same thing they told you," Clint said. "And made a point of telling me so."

"Well then," he said, "you must have been asking the right questions. Take some solace in that."

"What little there is."

"Thanks for breakfast."

"I thought you were paying."

Reed looked mildly surprised.

"Do law enforcement officials in America pay for their meals?"

"Not if they can help it."

Reed smiled for the first time since Clint had met him and said, "Just trying to make you feel at home, mate."

As the inspector left Clint called the waiter over and ordered another cup of coffee. He was determined to stay right where he was until the expo beckoned.

He was annoyed at himself for seeking someplace else to eat last night. He had just finished telling Inspector Reed that adults had to live in the real world, and last night he had fled from the real world, thinking that *not* eating here would enable him to stop thinking about Harriet.

Welcome to the real world, where murder existed and confusion was king.

The man entered the lobby, passing as he did Chief Inspector James Reed. He knew the chief inspector because his name had been in the newspaper, and because he had seen him around the hotel asking questions.

Well, there was one little fellow he wasn't going to be able to ask any more questions of.

Never again.

Now it was back to the proper business at hand— choosing the next victim; and in a hotel the size of The King's Arms, there were ample women to choose from, especially with the added attraction of the expo.

The man walked over to the poster that now adorned the lobby and read about the legend from the American West.

How very interesting.

Clint was finishing up his coffee when both Hyde-White and Standford came bustling into the dining room, obviously looking for him. When they saw him they hurried to his table.

"There you are," Hyde-White said accusingly.

"We've been looking for you," Standford said.

"The expo's about to start," the older man said.

"We need you now."

"Well, I *was* looking for the two of you," Clint said as they assisted him to his feet. "And nobody down there would let me in—"

"We must go now," Hyde-White interrupted.

"Yes, we have to make our opening remarks to get things started," Standford said.

Together they propelled him toward the door.

"Now remember, I said I wasn't giving any talks—"

"You don't have to talk," Hyde-White said.

"Just stand up there with us," Standford said.

"Looking like an American Legend of the West."

"A *Legend* of the American West," Standford said. "Get it right, Winston, for heaven's sake."

"Legend of the American West..." Hyde-White was muttering as they pushed Clint toward the double doors that led to the King's Hall.

What, he couldn't help thinking, have I gotten myself into?

EIGHTEEN

As far as Clint was concerned the opening of the expo was very well attended. He refused to take credit for that. After all, the poster had just been put into the lobby yesterday.

"My dear," he heard a heavy-set woman saying as she went by, "when I saw that an American legend, a *gunman*, was going to be here I insisted that Henry take me along."

"Where did you read it?"

"In the *Times*, dear," the woman said. "It was in the *London Times*!"

Oh, no, Clint thought, but he had to give Hyde-White and Standford credit. The two promoters had moved quickly and effectively.

He had stood on the dais with them as they made their opening remarks, welcoming the gun manufacturers from all over the world, thanking them for coming, and inviting everyone to study their exhibits.

Later in the day, they told everyone, there would be discussions on various aspects of gun manufacturing, which they were sure everyone would find fascinating.

"And speaking of fascinating," Hyde-White said

then, "I know you're all anxious to meet our guest. He is a late addition to our activities, but we are especially pleased that he accepted our invitation. Ladies and gentlemen, a true . . . legend of the American West, Clint Adams, the Gunsmith!"

The crowd applauded, and Clint wanted to find a small hole somewhere, climb in, and pull it closed behind him. He smiled as best he could and acknowledged the applause and then hurried off the dais.

First murder and now total embarrassment.

He hoped *something* would happen over the course of the next five days to make this all worth it!

In the back of the room the man watched with great interest as the Gunsmith was introduced. He recognized the man as the one the waitress had spent the night with—*that* night with. The same man that Scotland Yard had taken in for questioning that morning.

The Gunsmith.

Scotland Yard's number one suspect.

This could all get even more interesting than he had ever imagined.

Things were much too hectic that morning for Clint to do anything more than wander around the room, looking at the various displays. Later he would force one of the partners to introduce him to the Colt people.

He was also gratified to see that very few people were approaching to speak to him. In fact, many of them looked intimidated when he walked by, although he had heard that same heavy-set woman complain to her husband, Henry, "Why, he's not even wearing his gun!"

Blame Scotland Yard, lady, he thought, not me.

When it was coming up on one o'clock and the crowd had thinned out, supposedly to go to lunch, he started for the exit of the hall, only to be intercepted by a surprisingly spry Hyde-White.

"Where are you going?" the older man demanded.

"To lunch."

"But you're our star attraction!"

"Even star attractions have to eat, Winston," Clint said, using the man's first name for the first time. "Especially when they have a lunch date with a very lovely woman."

"Well, all right, all right," Hyde-White said. "But please, do make it fast, won't you?"

"As fast as I can without choking to death on my food, Winston," Clint said, patting the man's shoulder solicitously. "After all, you wouldn't want a *dead* main attraction, would you?"

NINETEEN

When he reached Lesley Anne Collins' office she asked if he minded if they left the hotel for lunch.

"It's the only way I'll be able to eat in peace," she said.

He readily agreed. Maybe that would keep Hyde-White and Standford from coming and dragging him off before he was finished.

He went to his room for his new coat and then met her in the lobby. As they went out the front door he noticed that the hotel store was now open. When they passed it he looked in through the window and saw that there was a different clerk behind the counter.

"See something you want?" Lesley asked.

"No," he said, "I was just noticing that there's a different man working in there today."

"You're very observant," she said. "Yes, the regular man didn't show up for work today. We had to find someone to take his place."

"Is he sick?"

"I don't know," she said. "We haven't heard from him. There's a little place that I like to eat in, but it's a fair walk."

He huddled inside his coat against the cold.

"I don't mind," he lied.

Actually, the place was worth the walk—or maybe it was the company. This was a totally different woman than the one he had first met, and he was very pleased with this new model.

She introduced him to something called shepherd's pie, which was a combination of meat and vegetables beneath a bed of mashed potatoes. He found it delicious.

In fact, he found *her* delicious.

They talked about him first, and he told her much the same story he'd told the inspector. When they got around to her, she surprised him with her candor. In fact, he seemed to be bringing that out in people today. First Inspector Reed, and now Lesley Anne Collins.

"I am spoiled," she said. "Spoiled rotten. I grew up wealthy, never wanted for anything, and it's ruined me as an adult." She laughed, brushing a lock of reddish hair away from her forehead and said, "In fact, it's ruined me as a human being."

"Why do you say that?"

"Because . . . I am a difficult person to like. I mean, I don't *try* to make people like me."

"You don't have to," he said. "People will either like you or they won't."

"Well, they don't," she said self-consciously.

"I like you."

She looked up at him then and said, "I know. I

like you, too. I liked you from the first."

"You could have fooled me."

"Well, growing up as I did has also made me a snob," she said. "And you *are* a guest of the hotel . . ."

"But you're here with me now."

"Yes, I am," she said, "and I'm not exactly sure how to act."

"Don't act," he said, reaching across the table and covering her hand with his. "Just be yourself. I like you very much this way."

She smiled in an embarrassed way, slid her hand away from his, and picked up her glass of water.

"You don't go out of your way to make people *dis*like you, do you?"

"I don't believe so."

"Well then, I don't think you have as much of a problem as you seem to think."

"Maybe not," she said thoughtfully.

Over tea—he decided to have tea at least *once* while he was here—he remembered what Harriet Carlyle had said about Lesley Anne.

"Did you know Harriet well?" he asked. "Harriet Carlyle?"

"You mean the poor girl who was killed?"

"Yes."

"No, not very well. I'm even more of a snob with the help than I am with the guests. I do hope they find the maniac who killed her."

"I'm sure they will," Clint said, thinking "maniac" was the right word for a man or a woman who would kill a woman—or anyone—like that.

They walked back to the hotel from lunch in silence, but halfway there Lesley Anne slipped her arm through his, and they walked the rest of the way like that.

Outside the hotel she stopped and said, "Perhaps I should go in first."

"Don't want to be seen with a guest?"

"Let's just say I shouldn't," she said. "It is not encouraged for the employees to fraternize with the guests. I could lose my job."

"I thought you were wealthy?"

"I am."

"Then why are you worried about losing your job?"

"Because it's this job that is going to help me get over my problem."

"Aw, really?" he said. "I thought I was going to do that."

She looked away shyly.

"Can we have dinner later this evening?"

"I would like that," she said, "but it would have to be out of the hotel."

"That's all right with me, Lesley."

"All right, Clint," she said. "We could meet at that same restaurant at seven-thirty, if that's all right?"

Clint didn't know what the schedule of the expo was, but at this point he didn't care.

"That's fine."

"I'll see you then." She smiled, touched his arm, and went inside.

He waited about five minutes and then entered the hotel himself.

Across the street the man watched them, laughing softly to himself.

TWENTY

Clint noticed that many of the men at the expo had women on their arms. As in the case of Henry, who had the heavy-set woman with him, it was obvious that some of them were wives. Others, however, were just as obviously *not* wives.

The second half of the day, people were still a bit too intimidated by Clint to approach him, but he rather enjoyed watching them. Eventually he was able to pick out the more wealthy men in attendance. They were as well dressed as any of the others, but they invariably had a young woman on their arm. Sometimes it seemed that the older the man was, the younger the woman was.

As the first day came to a close—at six P.M., to his delight—he saw Hyde-White and Standford approaching him with another man in tow. He was in his early forties, tall and fit, and very obviously American.

"Clint Adams," Standford said, "I would like you to meet George Cameron—a fellow American."

"Mr. Cameron," Clint said, shaking the man's hand.

"It's a pleasure, Mr. Adams," Cameron said. "It

seems odd that we'd have to come all this way to meet."

"I suppose that's true."

Clint looked at the two partners with curiosity.

"Mr. Cameron," Standford said, "is the representative in attendance from the Colt Company. I explained that you had asked to meet someone from Colt."

"Indeed I had," Clint said. "Mr. Cameron, could I buy you a drink?"

"Sounds good to me," Cameron said. "I would like to talk to you, too."

"Excellent," Hyde-White said. "We shall leave you in each other's hands."

"We can go to the saloon—or the pub, as they call it here," Clint said.

"I've just arrived today," Cameron said, "so why don't you lead the way?"

They went to the pub, had a few pints, and talked guns. Clint found it fascinating actually to talk about guns with someone from the most famous gun company in America.

Eventually Cameron worked the subject around to what he wanted to talk to Clint about.

"I'd like to come up with a new model for the Colt company for a handgun," Cameron said, "and I'd like to name it after you."

"After me?"

Cameron nodded.

"The Gunsmith model. We can work out the details later as to what size and caliber the gun would be, but we would need a written agreement between you and the company before we could go ahead."

"Mr. Cameron."

"George, please."

"George," Clint said. "I'm flattered, but—"

"Look, Clint," Cameron said. "I know this is sudden, and I know we're a long way from home. Why don't you take some time to think it over?"

"Well . . . all right."

"Tomorrow the Colts will arrive," Cameron said.

"Which ones?"

"A lot of them, I'm afraid."

"Why do you say that?"

"Well, I was a very young man when old Sam died, but the company ran much easier when he was alive. Now we have brother James, Sam the son, Sam the nephew, and everyone is trying to run the company at the same time. It makes for a lot of confusion at times."

"And you try to keep it going?"

"I do my best," he said. "I'm a vice-president in the company, but I still have no say over anyone whose last name is Colt."

"It must get pretty frustrating sometimes," Clint said, commiserating.

"A lot of the time," Cameron said. "If I didn't love the company . . . well, never mind that. Tell me about this murder I've been hearing about. A young woman was killed right outside the hotel?"

Clint filled Cameron in on Harriet Carlyle's death, leaving out his own involvement with the woman.

"Horrible," Cameron said.

Clint noticed the time and said, "I have a dinner

engagement, so if you'll excuse me . . ."

"Of course."

They both stood.

"It was a real pleasure talking to you," Clint said, shaking hands.

"Clint," Cameron said, grasping Clint's hand in both of his, "please think over my offer. We'll talk about it tomorrow."

"I'll give it a lot of thought, George."

It was after seven, and he had just enough time to get his coat and meet Lesley Anne at the restaurant.

TWENTY-ONE

Clint couldn't say that he *didn't* expect to end up in bed with Lesley Anne Collins—in fact, he had planned it, but he hadn't expected it to happen that night.

After dinner she had asked, "Do you have to go back to the hotel?"

"No," he's said. "I don't *have* to. Why?"

"I have a flat near here," she said. "An apartment, where I can get away from the hotel."

"Are you inviting me there?" he asked.

"I am."

And so they went . . .

Her body had been manufactured for bed.

He undressed her, caressing her skin with his hands and his lips. Her breasts were large and rounded, the nipples dark brown. When he kissed them she shuddered, and when he bit them she moaned.

He lowered her to her bed, where she waited, naked, while he undressed. He joined her and gathered her to him. He enjoyed the way her full breasts and thighs felt against him, the way her buttocks felt in his hands. She slid her hands down his body and took hold of his cock, stroking it gently.

"Please," she said. "I can't wait . . ." She pulled him toward her.

He slid one leg over her, mounted her, and entered with one quick lunge. She was wet, and he went in easily. She gasped as he began to move in and out of her, and she closed her mouth over his neck and moaned. When he came explosively she gave a tiny scream and rode the crest of her own orgasm . . .

Franz Schmidt was a representative of his own company, Schmidt International Arms, and as usual his wife, Hilda, had refused to accompany him on his business trip. He argued with her, of course, but could not sway her.

Luckily.

He chuckled as he watched the blonde head slide down between his legs. If the day ever came that he told Hilda *not* to come, she would have been the first one on the train. All he had to do was *insist* that she attend, and he was safe.

Schmidt was a robust fifty-five, and the girl who was sucking his cock like it was a candy stick was easily thirty years younger than he was.

He was a thickly built man, his body covered with hair, but he knew women liked him because he had a large cock. In keeping with the rest of him, it was thick rather than long, but women like this one usually had no trouble accommodating him, whether it be with their mouth or that hungry little animal between their legs.

This girl's name was Ilsa—or so he had been told

—and she claimed to be German. He did not particularly care whether she was or wasn't. She had firm, young flesh, heavy breasts, and an avid, talented mouth, and from the sounds she was making she obviously enjoyed her work.

Suddenly he was erupting into her mouth, and all other thoughts fled from his mind . . .

Himmel, he thought, it is like dying . . .

When Ilsa left the hotel she pulled her coat tightly around her. The money Herr Schmidt had paid her was pushed down into one of the pockets, and she still had her hand on it. She had asked if he wanted her back the next day, and the man had laughed and said, "of course."

She did not mind this one. He was clean, kept himself in good shape for a man his age, and he did have an impressive organ.

No, she didn't mind this work at all.

When she left the hotel she turned right, walking the same way Harriet Carlyle had walked.

She was going to pass the same alley.

She was going to suffer the same fate.

As the blonde girl came into view the man reached for her, closed his hand over her mouth, and dragged her into the alley. She was a big girl and strong as she fought him, but she had no chance for survival. He held her down with one hand and took the orange scarf from his pocket with the other. Deftly he looped the scarf around her neck and strangled her with it, then dropped her carelessly to the hard ground. He leaned over and tied the scarf around her neck and then left the alley.

Lesley Anne Collins sat astride Clint Adams, his penis buried inside of her. She was riding him hard, and despite the cold outside, they were both sweating. When they were done they would both feel the cold breeze drying them, but for now they were only aware of each other . . .

She pressed her hands to his chest and brought herself down on him hard, turning first one way and then the other, and when she came she threw her head back so far that she suddenly looked headless to him.

He closed his eyes and groaned as he ejaculated into her, and then she collapsed atop him, a heavy and not at all unpleasant weight.

He reached for the sheet blindly, found it, and pulled it over both of them.

"Cold, love?" she asked.

"I don't want you to *catch* cold."

"Mmm," she said. "Never. Not while I have you to lie with me."

He slid his hands over her back and down to her buttocks.

"Mmmm," she moaned, kissing his chest. "I love the way you touch me."

She lifted her chin, and they kissed deeply, tongues lashing.

"Oh!" she said.

"What?"

"I feel you . . ."

"Uh-huh."

"Coming back to life so soon?" she breathed against his mouth.

"I don't know," he said. "Why don't you take a look and see?"

Clint walked back to the hotel by way of the deserted Piccadilly Circus. He had slipped from bed while Lesley Anne slept. He knew that if he stayed any longer he would have had to awaken her, and she *was* a working woman who did not want to lose her job.

As he passed the hotel he became aware that he was abreast of the store. He stopped and looked in the darkened window. What was it that was bothering him? So an employee of the store had not shown up for work that day? What did that mean?

He wondered if the man would show up today.

He stopped in front of the hotel, and as the night doorman opened the door for him he waved the man away. Instead, he walked further, taking the route Harriet had taken the night she was killed. When he reached the alley he peered into the darkness, but could not see anything. He considered his next move and then stepped into the alley. He wanted to see if it was blind or if it came out onto the back street.

He was halfway down the alley, his eyes adjusting to the darkness, when he saw something. He stopped short and thought, Oh dear God, no.

He moved forward cautiously. Although he doubted it, there was a chance that the killer was still in the alley. He leaned over the woman and saw that she was young—and dead. Around her neck was a scarf, which he had no doubt would turn out to be silk.

He stood up and listened intently. Although he knew he was alone in the alley with the dead girl, he wished fervently for his gun and decided that the next time he saw Inspector Reed, he would demand it.

Except that the next time he saw Reed he would be telling him that *he* had found the body of a second girl.

Since he was the chief suspect in the case, how was that going to look?

TWENTY-TWO

"This does not look good," Chief Inspector James Reed said.

He was in the hotel manager's office with Clint. The girl's body had already been removed from the alley.

"Don't you think I knew that when I sent for you, Reed?" Clint said. "If I killed her, would I make it look like I found her?"

"I didn't say I thought you did it, Clint," Reed said. "I just said it doesn't look good."

"Has anyone identified her?"

"No," Reed said. "We've had several employees of the hotel take a look at her, but no one's been able to put a name to her yet. I don't think she works here at the hotel."

"A guest, then?"

"Perhaps."

"What was she doing out that late?"

"We'll never be able to ask her that."

Reed rubbed the corners of his mouth with his thumb and forefinger. "What am I going to do with you?" Reed asked aloud, although the question was really meant for himself.

"How about letting me go to sleep?"

"What were you doing on the street at three in the morning?"

"Coming back from a dinner engagement."

"*That* late?"

"The engagement stretched on," Clint said, hoping he wouldn't have to elaborate for the man.

Reed rubbed his mouth and said, "I see."

"Can I ask a few questions?"

"Why not?" Reed said. He sat down in a straight-backed chair. Clint had taken a seat behind the manager's desk.

"The killer in France three years ago."

"What about him?"

"How many girls did he kill?"

Reed frowned a moment, then said, "Five."

"And how much time passed between each murder?"

Reed sat up straight and said, "I don't know, but I will check. That's very good, Clint. If the time between the first two women is the same, then we might be able to figure out the time between the second and third."

"And you'll really know if you're dealing with a mimic killer."

"I'll attend to that right now."

"One other thing."

"What?"

"The scarves that were used were purchased here, right?"

"Yes," Reed said, taking the latest scarf from his pocket. It was orange, and he showed Clint the label near the stitched seam on the end.

"Well, the clerk who works there didn't show up for work today."

"Was he sick?"

"They didn't hear from him. He's the regular clerk, and they had to replace him."

Reed frowned.

"I'll send someone to his home to check on him. If he is missing, it might mean something."

"I agree," Clint said, standing. "I've got to get some sleep."

"I have to get back to the Yard."

They left the manager's office together. Outside, the night manager was huddling behind the desk with the night clerk.

"I need an address on the man who runs the hotel store," Reed said.

"He wasn't in today," the night manager said.

"I know that," Reed said. "I need his name and address."

"Do you think he is the killer?" the night manager asked anxiously.

Reed smiled tightly and said, "Sir, I would really like to get going."

"Yes, yes, of course," the man said. "I'll get the information for you."

As the night manager scurried into his office Clint said, "Brute."

"Don't you have somewhere to go?" Reed asked.

"Yes," Clint said, "to bed. See you in the morning—uh, that is, later today."

"We'll be seeing each other," Reed assured him.

• • •

In his room Clint thought about Chief Inspector James Reed. Was the policeman trying to put him off guard, or had he really changed his attitude toward him?

Clint knew that his opinion of the inspector had changed, especially after he learned about his experience with his ex-wife. Clint knew that a disastrous affair of the heart could push a man to the brink. What Reed had gone through was enough to . . . to what?

Clint felt a chill.

Was it enough to drive a man to murder?

The man had not expected the girl to be found so early. He found it interesting that it had been the Legend from America Clint Adams, who had found her. He had probably been coming back from his little tryst with the cold bitch from the hotel—except maybe she had heated up a little bit for *him*.

She was a whore, then, like all the others. She was therefore worthy of *him*, worthy of becoming one of his victims.

Maybe he'd save her for last.

The best for last.

Clint tried to sleep, but found that he could not. He kept thinking about Inspector Reed as a possible murder suspect. The man seemed genuinely dedicated to his work. Could a man like that be a killer?

Truly, *any* man could be a killer, but if Reed was telling the truth, in all his years as a policeman he had never killed anyone. Killing, then, was something totally alien to him.

And yet he himself had said that *some* people *enjoyed* killing. Had he somehow gotten a taste of it and found that he liked it too much to stop?

Or was Clint going too far out on a limb with this line of thinking? Maybe he was being totally unfair to a good policeman.

He tried to push the troubling thoughts from his mind and get to sleep.

Who knew what the morning—what the next few *hours*—might bring?

TWENTY-THREE

When Clint woke his eyes felt gritty, as if someone had sprinkled sand into them—real sand, not the kind children were told the sandman brought to them.

He rose, washed, and dressed and then remembered that he hadn't asked Reed to return his gun. Well, the situation had probably not been perfect for such a request. He was, after all, still the only legitimate suspect in the two murders. In fact, he himself realized that he was the only man to have had contact with both girls—even if his contact with the second girl had been only after she was dead.

Chief Inspector James Reed looked out the window of his office at Scotland Yard. He could see the Tower of London, but he wasn't looking at it, he was looking *past* it—or *through* it. He stood that way for a few moments, then shook himself and backed away from the window. He pressed the heels of his hands tightly against his eyes, which were burning and gritty. No sleep and not enough sleep, they both usually left his eyes gritty. He wondered if others felt the same as well.

He turned and looked at his desk, where his notebook was. He opened it to the page where he'd written the name of the missing store clerk.

The clerk's name was William Foxhall. Reed had gone to his home address, and there had been no answer at the door. He had then awakened the landlord and had him open the door for him. The man balked until Reed identified himself as an inspector from Scotland Yard.

Once inside the flat it was obvious that no one had been there for at least a couple of days. The man was not out sick; he was missing—but why? Did it have anything to do with the two murders? Maybe the man who bought the scarves was afraid the clerk would finally remember who he was.

Reed was going to have to go to the hotel and talk to the employees about Foxhall now. Maybe he had had some connection with one or both of the dead women.

And maybe his disappearance was just another matter entirely.

Just what he needed: another case.

He turned his notebook to the next page. There he had the sequence of the murders in France. One night between the first two murders, two nights between the second and third, and then the fourth and fifth on consecutive nights. All the murders in France had taken place at night, and the bodies were not discovered until the following morning. This second body had been discovered early because something had drawn Clint Adams into that alley, but they certainly had not gained any advantage from the extra hours.

They had two days to try and find this madman before he struck again.

When Lesley Anne Collins arrived at work early that morning, the first thing she heard about was the second murder.

She went to her office, feeling sick and angry. Sick because another young girl had been murdered, angry because all she had wanted to do today was bask in the afterglow of the night with Clint Adams. Now this ugliness had intruded on that.

She stared down at the top of her desk and decided just to go ahead and handle the day's work. The murders had nothing to do with her.

Nothing at all.

The man saw Lesley Anne Collins arrive for work and watched as she walked across the lobby, her stride long, purposeful, and graceful. She was better than either of the two girls he had killed so far, and she would be better than the next two.

After that it would be her turn.

TWENTY-FOUR

Hyde-White and Standford were obviously waiting for Clint when he came down the steps.

"Did you hear?" Hyde-White asked.

"I heard," Clint said, "if you're talking about the second murder."

"Dreadful thing," Standford said. "Dreadful."

Obviously they had no idea that he had found the body, and he didn't enlighten them.

"Are you ready?" Standford asked.

"For what?" Clint asked cautiously.

"Well, people will have gotten over their initial awe by now and will probably want to talk to you."

"If they want to talk, I'll be ready."

"I say, dear boy," Hyde-White said. "Wouldn't you think it advisable to wear your pistol?"

"I don't have my pistol," Clint said. "Scotland Yard relieved me of it."

"Well," Standford said, "there are plenty of guns around here. I'm sure we could get you one."

That didn't sound like a bad idea to Clint, but he had a condition.

"If you do get me one," he said, "make sure it isn't loaded."

"Not loaded?" Standford asked. "What good is a pistol if it is not loaded?"

"Do you expect me to have to shoot anyone here?" Clint asked.

"Well, of course not, but—"

"It will look just as real unloaded as loaded," Clint said. "Take my word for it."

"Very well," Standford said. "Why don't you mingle a bit? There are discussions going on in the adjacent room, if you are interested."

"I think I'll just walk around here and talk to some of the manufacturers."

"As you wish. We must leave you to yourself. We have errands to attend to."

"Take care of your expo, fellas," Clint said. "I'll be fine."

"Er," Hyde-White said, "you won't go away, will you?"

"No, Winston," Clint said. "I won't go away."

"Capital!"

After the partners had left him, he began to make a slow circuit of the room, stopping to talk to a manufacturer's representative when he saw something that interested him.

He suddenly remembered the offer George Cameron had made to him the day before, of Colt naming a model after him. He hadn't had time to think about it at all.

He looked around for the Colt display, but Cameron wasn't there, just a young man showing people some of the Colt lines. Clint wondered if any of the Colt family had arrived yet.

He noticed the man named Henry with his heavy-set wife, and the woman was giving Clint a critical going-over with her eyes. Finally she disengaged herself from her husband's arm and started to approach him. Her husband saw what she was doing and called out, "Grace!" but the woman ignored him and continued until she was face to face with Clint.

"I don't believe you really are the Gunsmith," she said huffily.

"And why is that, ma'am?"

"Why, you're not wearing a pistol. Everyone knows that a real cowboy wears a pistol, no matter where he goes."

"The fact of the matter is, ma'am, I am not a cowboy."

"You're not?" she asked, looking surprised.

"No, ma'am," he said. "I'm considered to be a killer."

"A . . . killer?" Her eyes went wide.

"Yes, ma'am, but you are right about one thing."

"What is that?" she asked, wary now.

"I should be wearing my gun, but I can explain why I am not."

"You can?"

"Have you heard of the two brutal murders of young girls that have taken place within the past three days?"

"Why, yes, of course—"

"You see," he said, leaning closer to her, "I am Scotland Yard's prime suspect."

"You . . . are . . . ?"

"And for that reason they have taken my gun from me."

"They . . . have . . . ?"

"But that doesn't matter," he went on. "You see, those girls were not shot, they were . . . *strangled*!"

"Oh," she said. "Oh dear . . . Henry . . ." She began to look around frantically for her husband, backing away from Clint. "Henry!"

Finally she turned and ran into the crowds of people, looking for her husband.

"What did you say to her?" a voice asked from behind him. "She looks as if she saw a ghost."

Clint turned and faced Inspector Reed.

"I told her I was a mad strangler," he said. "She was disappointed that I wasn't wearing my gun."

"I see."

"Have you been to bed yet?"

"Not yet," Reed said.

"I didn't sleep very well myself."

"I went to the missing man's flat," Reed said. "He hadn't been there for at least a couple of days."

"So he really is missing, then?"

"Apparently. I want to talk to some of the hotel employees about him."

"It might not even be connected with the murders," Clint said.

"Yes, I've thought of that. I almost hope it is. I'd hate to have to work on two cases at once. The murder should take priority."

Clint opined that the murderer might have been afraid that the clerk would eventually remember a man who bought a number of those silk scarves.

"I'd thought of that myself."

"I wonder if they keep any kind of written record on their customers."

"That's a good thought, Clint," Reed said. "I'll check on it."

"Just trying to be helpful."

"I know. Well, I'll leave you to your public. I see someone else coming after you."

Clint turned as Reed left and saw George Cameron approaching him with two men behind him.

Maybe he was finally going to meet some members of the famous Colt family.

TWENTY-FIVE

"Clint, so glad to see you," George Cameron said. They shook hands, and he said, "I'd like you to meet a couple of gents."

He turned and presented each man in turn.

The older man, white-haired, pink-skinned, sporting a pot belly, which made him appear shorter than he was, was James Colt, Samuel Colt's brother.

The younger man, tall, thin, slightly stooped, in his late thirties, was introduced as Samuel Jarvis Colt, the son of Sam Colt, who started the Colt company.

"I'm glad to meet you both."

"It's a real pleasure to meet you, Mr. Adams," Samuel Colt said. "I've done a lot of reading about your many exploits."

"I hope you don't believe them all," Clint said.

"No," Colt said, "but they make fascinating reading, and there must be some *basis* of truth."

"Some," Clint admitted, "but very little."

"You're modest."

James Colt spoke up now, and he was obviously less enamored of Clint's reputation.

"I understand George has approached you with an offer to name a Colt model handgun after you."

"He mentioned it, yes," Clint said. "I haven't really been able to think about it—"

"Well, I just want you to know that George did not consult the family before he made that offer—"

"I don't have to consult the family, James," George Cameron said, cutting the older man off. "I have the right to make these decisions."

"If this is going to be a problem—" Clint began.

"No, it's not going to be a problem," George said. "Don't worry about that, Clint. Gentlemen, why don't we go over to the display. Clint, we'll talk later."

"All right, George."

"Gentlemen? We should also meet our hosts."

As Cameron herded the Colts off, Clint was aware of a bitter disappointment after having met two of the family members. He wasn't looking forward to meeting any of the others if these two were representative.

If *they* didn't want a gun named after him, then *he* certainly didn't want it.

He was suddenly sorry he had come to the expo, and he did something he had told Winston Hyde-White he wouldn't do.

He turned and left.

When he reached the lobby he started to head for the saloon, but decided to detour and stopped at Lesley Anne's office. If she wasn't alone, he wouldn't bother her. Luckily, as he entered he found her alone.

"Good morning," he said.

She looked up from her desk and smiled.

"Good morning. How are you?"

"Tired. I didn't sleep very well."

"I slept *very* well," she said. "I'm so sorry you didn't."

"Well, I had an excuse," he said. "You heard about the second murder?"

"Yes," she said. "It's ghastly."

"I found her."

"You found the second girl?" There was sympathy in her voice as she stood up and moved to him. "I'm so sorry. It must have been horrible."

She touched him, then remembered where they were and put her hands at her sides.

"Did you know her?"

"No, I never saw her before."

"Has Scotland Yard been able to identify her?"

"Not yet. They're thinking that she may have been a guest of the hotel and not an employee."

Lesley Anne frowned. "I heard she was a prostitute."

"She might have been."

"Then she would not have been a guest of this hotel."

"Your snobbery is showing."

"Perhaps," she said, backing off only a bit, "but we do not allow prostitutes here."

"Not to take rooms themselves, but men come in with women who are not their wives." He got an idea suddenly and talked it out. "I saw a lot of men at the expo with women on their arms, some of them young women."

"Perhaps she was with one of them?"

"Maybe," he said. "I have to find the inspector. He's somewhere in the hotel."

He stuck his head out into the hall, saw that no one was coming, and then went back in and kissed her quickly.

"You can do better than that," she said and kissed him hard.

"I'll talk to you later," he said, pushing her away, when he would rather have pulled her to him. "I have to find the inspector and talk to him about something."

TWENTY-SIX

Clint started working his way through the hotel, trying to find Inspector Reed. He finally found him talking to someone in the catering department.

"Looking for me, or planning to cater a private party?" Reed asked.

"Let's go for a walk."

Reed thanked the man he'd been talking to, who went back to chopping lettuce.

Out in the hall Clint said, "I just thought of something."

"What?"

"I think the woman I found today was with one of the men attending the expo."

"You saw her?"

"No, but I saw plenty of women like her."

"Are we talking about prostitutes?"

"We are," Clint said.

"These men are attending this expo with prostitutes?"

"Look," Clint said. "You know Hyde-White and Standford, so tell me if I'm wrong. They are a couple of real promoters, operators. Am I right?"

"You are," Reed said. "I might even go so far as to say they are a couple of con men."

123

"Then how did this expo come about?"

Reed shrugged as they started down a flight of stairs to the lobby.

"I checked this out," he said, "and it appeared to be legitimate. I mean, these *are* real gun manufacturers, aren't they?"

"They are," Clint said. "Now, would they have any trouble supplying prostitutes for the single men or the men who are attending alone?"

"None at all," Reed said, "but we can't have every man who is attending alone take a look at the body. We'd have a line around the block—"

"Not everyone," Clint said, touching his arm. "Just the two of them, Hyde-White and Standford."

Reed nodded and said, "All right, I'll take them now and let them have a look at her. Hopefully they know all the girls they hired."

"They're going to squeal about being taken away from their expo," Clint said.

"That will be too bad."

"Well," Clint said, "you could take one of them and leave the other behind."

Reed frowned.

"Hyde-White said he knew you when you were a kid."

"Yes," Reed said. "He was like an uncle to me. In fact, he wanted to teach me to be . . . like him."

"A con man?"

"Yes. I think he was disappointed when I went the other way."

"They're likable old guys."

"I know they are," Reed said. "Maybe if this venture is successful they will go straight."

Clint caught Reed's eyes and said, "What is that saying about teaching old dogs new tricks?"

"I don't know," Reed said. "It must be an Americanism. I will let you know what happens."

They completed the descent to the lobby, and then Reed continued down to where the expo was being held.

On a whim Clint walked over to the store and entered. The young man behind the counter smiled and said, "Can I help you?"

"No," Clint said. "No, I'm just looking around."

"Are you a guest of the hotel?"

"Yes."

"We have some lovely items I could show you—"

"No, thank you." Suddenly Clint noticed that this man looked a little like the other man. Same general age and coloring, a little taller, but not noticeably so.

"Tell me, do you usually fill in when the other man—what was it, Foxhall—is out?"

"Often, but not always."

"But often?"

"Yes."

"Why couldn't they find you yesterday?"

"It was my day off, but they sent someone to my home to get me."

"Do you have those silk scarves?"

"Oh, those," the man said. "No, Scotland Yard took whatever we had so we couldn't sell any more. I'm sorry. Did you want them?" Suddenly the man's look became wary, and he stammered, "W-why did you want them?"

"Relax," Clint said. "I'm not the killer. I'm working with the Yard." It wasn't the truth, but it was close enough not to be a lie.

The man relaxed noticeably.

"Do you remember selling more than one scarf to anyone at any time when you were working?"

The man thought a moment, then said, "No, I can't say that I do."

"Well, if something does come to you, would you notify Inspector Reed of the Yard, or myself. My name is Clint Adams; I'm a guest."

"All right, sir. I'll do that."

"Thank you."

Clint left the store. It was just a long shot, but if the killer was smart enough, he would have bought as many scarves as he needed, and he would have bought them separately, so no one would remember.

If he was smart. Clint Adams had known a lot of dumb killers in the past.

He only hoped they were dealing with one now.

The man frowned as he saw Inspector Reed and Clint Adams together in the lobby of the hotel. They did not look like a policeman and someone who was under suspicion for murder. They looked too friendly.

When they separated the inspector went downstairs, and Clint Adams went into the hotel store.

Suddenly the man didn't find Clint Adams so interesting anymore.

Suddenly he saw Adams as a threat—an even more threatening figure than the inspector. At least the man understood policemen.

He did not understand legends of the American West at all.

But that didn't mean he couldn't kill one.

TWENTY-SEVEN

Clint relented and spent the rest of the day at the expo. He left once more, to ask Lesley Anne if she could have lunch with him, but she was too busy. They agreed to meet for dinner at the same restaurant.

As it turned out, some of the awe *had* worn off, and he was approached by several people who wanted to talk about America. The few who wanted to talk about his "exploits," he tried to satisfy by talking about Wild Bill Hickok, Bat Masterson, and Wyatt Earp. He talked about everyone and everything—except himself.

At one point he saw Standford walking around the room alone and went over to him.

"Where's your partner?" he asked.

"That young whippet took him away to show him some dead chippie," Standford complained. "Now I've got to keep all these people happy alone."

"Can't you do without him for a while?"

Standford made a face.

"Winston is the social one."

"And you're the one with the business sense?"

He scowled and looked around.

"Tell me something, Edward," Clint said. "Who hired the prostitutes, you or Winston?"

Standford stared directly at Clint.

"Reed and I have been talking."

"Are you working with the Yard on these murders?' he asked. Clint could see an idea forming in his devious little mind.

"No, Edward, I'm not. I'm not a detective, but I am getting tired of dead bodies, especially when I trip over one."

"What are you talking about?"

"I found the second body."

"How dreadful for you."

"It could be dreadful for you."

"How so?"

"If the girl was one of the prostitutes you hired, Reed will have some questions."

"We don't know anything about the girls," Standford said. "We were just trying to keep some of the out-of-town manufacturers happy. You know, the ones who were attending on their own."

"I can understand that, Edward."

"You can?"

"Sure, but you had better hope Winston can identify her."

"Why?"

"Because if he can't, Reed will have to march every manufacturer you were trying to keep happy past a dead body to see if they can identify her. They might not be too happy after that parade."

Standford rubbed his hand over his face.

"Winston should be able to identify her. We only hired seven girls."

"I hope that doesn't burn up too much of your profits," Clint said.

Standford took a pocket watch from his vest and said, "I have to wrap up one of the sessions."

"See you later, Edward."

Standford went off to break up his session, and Clint turned back to the crowded room. As he did he saw George Cameron coming toward him.

"Clint, Clint," the man said. "I'm so sorry about what happened."

"That's all right, George," Clint said. "But under the circumstances, I don't think it would be advisable to go ahead with—"

"No, no," Cameron said. "Don't say that yet. I want you to think over my offer very carefully before you make a final decision."

"But if James Colt is against it—"

"I have more to say about it than he does," Cameron assured him. "Please, think about it some more."

"All right, George," Clint said after a moment. "I'll give it some more thought."

"Thanks," Cameron said. "I appreciate it. I have to run. I want to talk with a German manufacturer about something."

Clint nodded, and the man went off. He found that he liked George Cameron a lot less than he had initially. In some ways, he was as much an operator as Hyde-White and Standford, but without their charm.

As the day's activities came to a close, Clint made sure he was the first one out of the room and up the stairs to the lobby. It was six P.M., and he had to meet Lesley Anne for dinner at seven-thirty. He wondered if Reed was still in the hotel, or if he had left long ago. He also wondered why he still had not asked the man for his gun back. Perhaps he was getting used to not wearing it, after all these years of having it hanging on his hip or within easy reach.

Idly he wondered what had happened to the partners' plan to get him a gun, albeit an empty one.

The man watched the expo people filing out and took special note of the ones who had women on their arms. Also, he took special interest in those couples who went directly to the dining room. Of course, his victims would be those young ladies who stayed in the hotel, either as guests or as the "guest" of a guest.

Because Clint Adams and Inspector Reed seemed to be working together, the man decided that he had to update his schedule.

He was going to take his next victim tonight, and whoever she was, she had Reed and Adams to thank for it.

"Mr. Adams?"

Clint turned at the sound of the voice and found

himself facing a man he had never seen before.

"Yes?"

"Scotland Yard, sir," the man said, showing Clint his identification. Clint didn't think that was the smartest thing to do right in the lobby of the hotel. "Sergeant Charles."

"Hello, Sergeant," Clint said. "What can I do for you?"

"Inspector Reed's compliments. He asked me to look you up," the sergeant said. "He wanted me to inform you that we would have a man in the hotel starting tomorrow, and one watching the alley where both women were killed."

"Tomorrow night?"

"Yes. That is when we expect the next, er, attempt."

"I see. Well, thank Inspector Reed for keeping me informed, will you?"

"Yes, sir, I will."

As the sergeant left the lobby, Clint wondered about Reed's decision to let him in on his plans.

Maybe he had officially been passed from the suspect list—which probably left it quite empty.

Franz Schmidt was dining alone, but he was too nervous to eat.

Ilsa had still not appeared, and he had heard the stories about a girl being murdered outside the hotel during the night. He wondered if it could possibly be Ilsa who had been killed, and he also wondered if he should talk to Scotland Yard about it.

If he did talk to the police, there was always the chance Hilda would hear about it, and then what was he to do?

Still, if the dead girl *was* Ilsa, he wanted to do something to help the police catch her killer.

He looked up from his table, and from where he was seated he was able to look right out into the lobby. Directly in his line of sight was the man from America, Clint Adams, the one they called the Gunsmith.

He stood up and walked hurriedly toward the lobby.

TWENTY-EIGHT

Clint was about to go to his room to freshen up, when he heard his name again. This time it was spoken with a heavy German accent. He turned and saw a rather thick-bodied man in his fifties approaching him.

"Can I help you?" Clint asked.

It was obvious that the man was nervous. He kept moistening his lips with his tongue, and his eyes kept darting back and forth.

"Herr Adams," the man said. "I am attending the expo, and this is why I know your name."

"And what is your name?"

"I am Franz Schmidt."

Clint remembered seeing a display booth with the name Schmidt on it.

"What can I do for you, Mr. Schmidt?"

"Ah, is there someplace we can talk, please?" the man asked. "I, uh, I very much need your help, Herr Adams."

"We could go inside for a drink."

"Uh, something a little less public, perhaps?" the man said.

"I was about to go to my room and freshen up for

135

dinner," Clint said. "Would you like to come up with me?"

"That would be fine."

"Come along, then."

The nervous man trailed Clint to his room and didn't seem any less nervous when they were safely inside.

Clint removed his jacket and shirt and said, "You can talk while I wash up."

"I do not know what to do," the man said, his tone anguished.

"About what?"

"The girl who was murdered."

Clint stopped short of rubbing his wet hands over his face. "What about her?"

"I am afraid it might be . . ."

"Might be who?"

"Herr Adams, I am a married man . . ."

That made it clear enough. Schmidt was one of the lonely manufacturers who had ended up with one of the whores supplied by Hyde-White and Standford.

"I understand, Mr. Schmidt."

"Do you?" Schmidt asked hopefully.

"Yes," Clint said. "Please continue."

"I was with a woman last night in my room. A remarkable young woman, very blonde and—"

"Could we get to the point please, Mr. Schmidt?" Clint remembered that the second dead girl was a young blonde.

"Yes, of course," Schmidt said. "I was supposed

to see her again today, but she has not appeared. I am afraid . . . afraid . . ."

"Afraid that she may be the girl who was killed?"

"Yes."

"And if you come forward and identify her, your wife might find out?"

"Yes," Schmidt said, this time explosively, because it now became obvious that Clint *did* indeed understand. "You see why I need help?"

"Mr. Schmidt," Clint said, drying his hands, "it may not be necessary for you to come forward. Someone might have identified the girl today."

"Truly? Was it . . . was it her?"

"I don't know the outcome, yet," Clint said. "There is a possibility that she was *not* identified. If you are needed, I can assure you that your name will be kept in the strictest confidence. Scotland Yard would be satisfied to have her identified. They would have no need to . . . embarrass you."

"Truly?" Schmidt said, his gratitude plain on his face. "You can guarantee this?"

"No," Clint said. "I can't guarantee it, but I feel certain that that will be the case. Why don't you just leave yourself in my hands? I know the inspector who is investigating the murders, and I will speak to him in the morning."

"How wonderful," Schmidt said happily. "Herr Adams, I cannot tell you how grateful—"

"That's quite all right, Mr. Schmidt. Why don't you go and get yourself some dinner and relax."

"Yes, well," the man said, touching his ample stomach, "I do feel my appetite returning."

The man turned, opened the door, then looked at Clint again and said, "Again, my gratitude—"

Clint waved him away and said, "Think nothing of it. Thank you for speaking candidly to me."

"Yes," the man said. "Yes," and he left.

After Herr Schmidt had left Clint sat down and thought about it. He knew he had overstepped his bounds, but then he hadn't actually made any hard promises to Franz Schmidt. Hopefully he'd be able to convince Inspector Reed to keep the man's name a secret if it became absolutely necessary to use him to identify the dead girl.

He finished cleaning up, put on a fresh shirt, put his jacket back on, donned his new coat, and left to meet Lesley Anne for dinner.

On the way out he decided that he was *not* used to being without his gun.

He still felt pretty damned naked without it.

TWENTY-NINE

He picked out his victim and, in a daring move, decided to kill her inside the hotel instead of waiting for her to leave. Besides, she might have been one of those all-night prostitutes.

He watched her leave the dining room on the arm of an older man. If he remembered correctly, the man was a gun manufacturer from Sweden. He found out the man's room number and then bided his time.

Over dinner Lesley Anne said, "I'm sorry."

"About what?"

"About being a snob again this morning. You know, about the dead girl. I know it must have been horrible for you, finding her like that."

"It wasn't very pleasant," he said, but something in his voice must have struck her as odd.

"Then again, you have seen a lot of bodies, haven't you?"

"More than my share."

"Were you shocked when you found her?"

"Disgusted would be more like it."

She picked at her dinner and then said, "Dead bodies don't frighten you, do they?"

"Live people frighten me, Lesley, not dead ones. We have nothing to fear from the dead, do we?"

"I've never seen a dead body."

"You're not missing anything."

After dinner they walked back toward the hotel. When he had met her at the restaurant she had apologized and told him that she had to work late that night. He assured her that he understood.

Now she said again, "I'm sorry I have to work."

"That's all right," he said. "I'm disappointed, but I understand."

She took his arm, gave it a squeeze, and said, "I'm disappointed, too." She held his arm until they reached the block of the hotel and then released it.

"I'm sorry about this sneaking around," she said at the door.

He smiled.

"Maybe some night you'll surprise me and sneak up to my room."

She grinned and said, "Maybe I will."

While she went inside he stood outside, wondering if he should walk down to the alley again. He decided against it, especially if Reed had a man watching it. It wouldn't look good.

Again.

The man watched Lesley Anne Collins walk across the lobby and once again marveled—as always—at the way she moved. At one time he had thought it might be nice to try to take her to bed.

Sex had never been as good for him, though, as killing.

Pity.

Clint entered the hotel and started across the lobby. Halfway across, he saw Reed sitting on one of the divans. The man stood up and intercepted him.

"Drink?" Reed asked.

"Why not?" Clint said. "It's still early."

"Identify the girl?" Clint asked when they were sitting in the pub with a pint each.

"Hyde-White verified that she was one of the girls they hired," Reed said. "He couldn't remember her name, though. He said Standford wouldn't, either."

"You need her name, huh?"

"We would like to notify her family, if she has any," Reed said.

"I . . . may be able to help."

Reed looked at him curiously.

"How?"

Clint told him a story about a man who had come to see him with a problem. He was careful not to mention Schmidt's name.

Not yet, anyway.

"Did you make him any promises?" Reed asked.

Clint shook his head.

"I didn't feel qualified to do that."

"Good," Reed said. "I can try to keep his name quiet, but I can't make any promises."

"He knows that."

"Who is he?"

"One of the manufacturers attending the expo," Clint said. "Franz Schmidt. He has a display downstairs. You'll be able to find him there in the morning."

"No," Reed said. "If we're going to try and keep this quiet I'll just go to his room early and ask him to come to the Yard."

It was evident that Reed would do his best to avoid embarrassing Schmidt.

"By the way. . ." Clint said.

"Yes?"

"I have a question."

"About what?"

"My gun."

"Oh," Reed said. "You want it back."

"I would like it back, yes."

"How have you felt walking around without it all this time?"

"Naked."

"I've never worn a gun. Is it heavy?"

"Not once you get used to it."

Reed shook his head and said, "How do you get used to it?"

Clint didn't want to get into another gun discussion with the inspector, so he held his tongue.

"Come to the Yard tomorrow," Reed said, standing up. "I'll give it back to you then."

"Does that mean I'm officially off the suspect list?" Clint asked.

"It would appear so," Reed said and left.

Clint stared after the inspector and realized that he

hadn't seriously thought about him as the killer since that thought had initially come to him. He discarded the idea for good, now. The man seemed to be doing his best to find the killer, getting very little sleep in the process.

Clint thought about going back to his room, but decided it was too early. He ordered another beer and wondered if they played poker in London.

THIRTY

Arne Beck was perhaps the best known gun manufacturer in Sweden. He was also possibly the homeliest man in all of Sweden. Still, Andrea Glover
thought, he was also one of the wealthiest men in
Sweden, and in her book, the third made up for the
second, and the first mattered not at all.

Andrea was slightly over the hill for the work she
was doing—in her thirties—but then Beck, who was
fifty-two, *had* requested a more mature woman. He
did not feel comfortable when they were *too* young.
He was single, but he still felt it was important to
keep up a dignified front. It wouldn't do for him to
walk around with a twenty-year-old on his arm—or
in his bed.

He and Andrea had gone right to bed after dinner,
and they were there when the knock came at the
door.

"Who could that be?" Andrea asked. "Your wife?"
She was teasing.

"I am not married," he said, frowning. "I will
send them away."

He got up out of bed, and Andrea watched his fat
ass waddle to the door. He was the unfortunate pos-

sessor of the biggest ears, the biggest nose, *and* the biggest ass she had ever seen on a man.

"Who is there?" he demanded loudly.

"Room service."

He turned to look at Andrea and shrugged. She shrugged back, which made her large breasts jiggle. Beck wanted nothing more than to dive back into bed with her and bury his face between those breasts.

"I ordered nothing!"

"Compliments of the hotel, sir."

"What is it?"

"Champagne."

"Ooh," Andrea said from the bed. "I love champagne. It makes me feel all tingly inside."

"Just a minute," Beck called out. He looked around frantically, then grabbed a towel and held it in front of him while he opened the door.

"Champagne," the bellboy said, showing Beck the bottle inside the bucket of ice. The bottle was a magnum, the largest bottle of champagne Beck had ever seen.

"May I bring it inside?" the bellboy asked.

"No," Beck said. "I will take it."

He reached for the bucket, saw that he would need two hands for it, and let the towel drop.

"Enjoy it, sir," the bellboy said and left without waiting for a tip.

Beck kicked the towel away, closed the door, and brought the champagne to the bed.

"Ooh," Andrea said, jumping to her knees. Again her breasts danced and jiggled. "Let's drink it right from the bottle, Arne."

He hurriedly opened the bottle, and when the cork popped, the champagne gushed out and struck Andrea right in the chest, dousing her breasts. Her nipples immediately became hard, and she laughed and sipped from the bottle, while Beck cleaned her breasts with his tongue.

The man waited until he felt sure they had both drunk the champagne and then made his way up to the third floor, where Arne Beck's room was. Using a skeleton key, he let himself into the room.

It was evident from the breathing and snoring that came from the bed that they had both consumed the entire bottle of champagne and were now soundly asleep. The room smelled of sex and sweat, and the man wrinkled his nose as he approached the bed. That was another reason why he preferred killing women to sleeping with them. It was so much cleaner, more sanitary.

The man was lying on his side, facing away from the woman. She was lying on her back, a large naked breast sagging to each side. He was mildly surprised to find that she was the one doing the snoring.

He took a silk scarf from his pocket, this one red. He took hold of her hair and pulled her head off the pillow so he could wrap the scarf around her neck. Her eyes fluttered sleepily, but by the time they opened the scarf was already tightening around her neck. She opened her mouth to scream, but no sound came out except for a low gurgle, which her bed partner could not hear. The man kept the pressure on the scarf until the woman's tongue protruded obscenely and her eyes had rolled up into her head. He released the pressure then and knotted the scarf around her throat.

As he stepped away from the bed he didn't see the champagne bottle on the floor. He stepped on it, and his ankle twisted. He swore loudly, and the man on the bed stirred. The killer waited, keeping still, hoping he would not have to kill the man, too. He derived no pleasure from killing men.

Finally the man settled back into his sleep, and the killer made his way quickly to the door, letting himself out. His ankle throbbed painfully as he left the third floor.

THIRTY-ONE

When Clint Adams woke that morning, it was with some disappointment. When he'd returned to his room the night before he'd been hoping that there would be a knock on his door soon after, and Lesley Anne Collins would sneak sweetly into his bed. It had not happened, and he'd fallen asleep waiting.

He had stayed in the pub for some time drinking pints, and his mouth felt like someone had sprinkled lye into it. He tried unsuccessfully to moisten it, then went to the pitcher and bowl on the dresser. He washed his face and sipped some water into his mouth while doing so.

He wondered if Reed had taken Schmidt to the Yard yet and decided simply to go there himself as soon as he was dressed. He wanted to find out if the girl had been properly identified, and most of all he wanted to pick up his gun.

When Lesley Anne Collins awoke in her bed she was saddened to find that she was alone. She had dreamed of Clint Adams, and consequently had thought he was there with her. When she awoke and found that he wasn't, she cursed herself for being too cowardly to sneak up to his room. If she lost her job,

149

though, she was sure she'd go back to being the insufferable snob that she had been before.

She reclined in the bed on her back for a moment, running her hands over body and thinking of Clint Adams. She shook herself then, rose, and dressed for work.

Tonight she would not work late. Tonight they would make up for lost time.

When the man woke that morning he did so with a great sense of accomplishment. He knew that the Yard had a man watching the outside of the hotel, as well as one inside, and he had still gotten to his chosen victim with no problem.

Three down, one to go . . . and then the lovely Lesley Anne Collins.

When he stood up from bed he found his ankle tender, but he was able to put his weight on it. A small price to pay for the sense of power he felt.

Murder *was* so invigorating.

He could not imagine how he had lived without it all those years.

Arne Beck rolled over in bed to face Andrea Glover. He moaned and reached out for her, found one large breast, and cupped it. He pinched the nipple, then pinched it again, but she did not respond. That was odd, because she had the *most* sensitive nipples he'd ever encountered.

He squeezed her entire breast then, but still there was no response. It was then that he became aware that her skin was rather cold.

Then and only then did Arne Beck open his eyes. He found himself looking into the bulging eyes and protruding tongue of Andrea Glover—and the eyes were all whites!

"God, oh God!" Arne Beck cried out, leaping from the bed. He stopped there to look at her again and then, heart pounding, panic threatening to choke him, he turned and ran from the room, totally naked.

He was quite a sight when they saw him in the lobby.

By that time Clint Adams had already left the hotel and was on his way to Scotland Yard.

THIRTY-TWO

When Clint arrived at the Yard he was told that Chief Inspector Reed would be with him shortly. Fifteen minutes later he was taken to Reed's office. On Reed's desk was Clint's gun and holster.

"Take it," Reed said.

Clint moved to the desk and picked up the gun.

"Please do not wear it to stroll down Piccadilly."

"I won't. Did you bring Schmidt in?"

"Yes," Reed said. "He identified the girl as Ilsa Buckholz."

"Family?"

"He didn't know anything about that, but we're checking."

"Were you able to keep Schmidt's name clear?"

"Yes," Reed said, "Herr Schmidt will suffer no embarrassment as a result of his cooperation."

"Did you get any sleep last night?"

"An hour or so," Reed said, rubbing his face with both hands. "I'm going to send more men to the hotel tonight. If he's going to strike tonight, I want to catch him. I don't want any more women dying."

"Neither do I," Clint said. "If there's anything I can do—"

"You've done enough," Reed said. "This will

153

have to be a Yard operation. I wouldn't be able to use you and justify it to my superiors."

"I understand. Have you time for some breakfast?"

Reed shook his head.

"I've got to pick out the men I'm going to use tonight and make sure they're all available. Wives and girlfriends and such have to be consulted."

"That's decent of you."

Reed waved Clint's words away.

"Well, I'll see you later then, at the hotel."

"Undoubtedly."

As Clint moved to the door it opened, and a man stuck his head in.

"Inspector?"

"Yes?" Reed said, looking at the man wearily.

"Bad news, sir."

"Well, spit it out, man!"

"Another girl's been murdered. You're wanted at the hotel."

Clint looked at Reed and said under his breath, "Sonofabitch. He struck a night early."

Reed exploded out of his seat and said viciously, "Cheeky bastard!"

THIRTY-THREE

When they arrived at the hotel they were met by a bobby who had been called into the lobby when the naked Mr. Beck had started running around yelling, "Murder!" and "Help!" Also present were the men Reed had assigned to watch the inside and outside of the hotel.

"What the hell happened?" he demanded of the three policemen.

"The cheeky bugger sneaked into one of the rooms and strangled the girl while she slept in bed next to a man," one of the policemen said.

"And he didn't hear anything?" Reed demanded.

"Not a thing, sir."

"What's his name?"

"Beck," the policeman said, reading it from his notebook. "Arne Beck, from Sweden."

"Where is Mr. Beck?"

"He's in the manager's office," the officer said. "Uh, Inspector, he was naked, and he wouldn't go back to his room to dress."

"All right," Reed said. He looked at the bobby and said, "Get back out on the street."

"Yes, sir."

155

He looked at one of his officers and said, "I don't want the body touched until I see it."

"Yes, sir."

When neither of them moved Reed said, "Well, go upstairs and stay with it."

"Yes, sir!" they both said and hurried away.

"Come along," Reed said to Clint. "You might as well hear this."

Clint followed Reed to the manager's office, where they found a fat man wearing what appeared to be a tablecloth around him. He had the homeliest face Clint had ever seen.

"Mr. Beck?"

The man looked up at Reed with eyes that still reflected his shock.

"Please, sir," Reed said. "Tell me what happened."

Clint knew Reed was keyed up, and yet he was able to speak gently to the other man. Clint admired him for that quality.

Beck spoke in halting English and told them what he had found when he had awakened that morning.

"Tell me what happened last night."

"We had dinner," the man said. "After dinner we went to my room . . . to bed. Later, there was a knock on the door, and room service delivered a large bottle of champagne."

"Had you ordered champagne?" Clint asked.

"No, but the bellboy said that it was, um, compliments—is that what you say?"

"Compliments of the house?" Reed said.

"Yes," Beck said. "Exactly."

"Mr. Beck, we will have your room cleaned up as soon as possible, and then you can collect your belongings. Perhaps you'd like another room for the rest of your stay?"

"That would be kind."

Reed looked at the day manager, who was also in the room, and said, "Can you take care of that?"

"Yes, of course."

"Before we leave," Clint said to Beck, "can you describe this bellboy?"

The Swede did his best, and the description fit Jeffery perfectly.

"All right, Mr. Beck," Reed said. "Thank you. Try to relax now."

"Yes, yes, I will try."

Clint and Reed went outside.

"The killer sent the champagne," Clint said when they were in the lobby.

Reed rubbed at the corners of his mouth.

"It could have been drugged."

"It wouldn't have to be," Clint said. "A man, a woman, a bottle of champagne. They'd be asleep soon enough, just as if they *were* drugged."

"She was killed right next to him in bed, and he didn't see or hear anything," Reed said, shaking his head. "Amazing."

"Like you said," Clint said. "Our man has a lot of gall." Clint had been able to guess that was what "cheeky" meant.

"To say the least," Reed said. He took a deep breath and then said, "Do you want to come up?"

"I think I'll pass on viewing the body," Clint said.

"I'll look around for the bellboy who delivered the bottle of champagne."

"You know him?"

"The description rings a bell."

"All right. I'll meet you back here."

"Right."

As Reed started to walk away Clint said, "Reed."

"Yes?"

"The killer had access to room service, and he must have had a key to get into the room."

"I agree."

"You know what that means?"

Reed nodded. "There's a good chance he works for the hotel."

"Maybe we're finally getting somewhere."

"I hope so," Reed said. "There are still two women out there who are in danger."

"Yeah," Clint said.

"Oh, and do me a favor, will you?"

"What?"

Reed pointed to the gun and holster Clint was still holding and said, "Put that away?"

THIRTY-FOUR

Clint went up to his room to put his gun away, but it didn't sit right with him that he was going looking for a killer without one. He finally decided to stick the gun in his pants at the small of his back. It was bulky there, but Reed had no experience spotting weapons on a man, and it might pass.

He went back downstairs and asked the clerk where Jeffery was.

"He worked late," the clerk said. "He must be getting dressed to go home."

"Where do the bellboys dress?"

"There's a room in the back. Go through that door that says *Employees Only* and walk to the end. There are two doors. They dress in the room to the right."

"Thank you."

Clint left the desk and headed for the door, nodding to a few people who had arrived for the expo, which would open at ten.

Abruptly the man realized something.

In his haste to take his third victim, the man had made a mistake, and he knew it. The bellboy could

159

identify him. He had to make sure that didn't happen.

Clint went through the door marked *Employees Only* and walked down the long hall. He found the two doors the clerk had spoken of and opened the one on the right.

"Jeffery?"

There was no answer, and he didn't hear any sounds in the room. He stepped inside and closed the door behind him.

The room was long, and there were gas lamps on the walls. There were rows of stalls, which he assumed were used by the bellboys to store their clothing and possessions when they came to work.

"Jeffery," he called again. "Is anyone here?"

He looked down the first row of stalls, then moved to the second row.

That was when he saw him, lying face down on the floor.

Quickly, he moved to the man, in case he was still alive. As he bent over him, Jeffery's stall suddenly toppled over onto both of them. As Clint was struggling to get out from under it he heard footsteps, and then he heard the door open and close. Finally he got free and ran to the door. He opened it, gun in hand, and ran down the hall out into the lobby. Several people gasped when they saw him holding his gun and pulled away from him.

He ran to the desk and said, "Did anyone come running out here just now?"

"N-no," the desk clerk said, nervously eying the gun.

"Damn!" Clint said. "Where does the other door in the back lead to?"

"A hallway."

"To where, man?"

"Outside, ou-outside."

"Why didn't you tell me that before? Have someone find Inspector Reed, and get him down here!"

He turned and ran back to the door marked *Employees Only*. As he did he passed Henry's wife, the heavy-set woman, and when she saw his gun in his hand she said, "Well, it's about time!"

Clint rushed back down the hall, went through the door on his left, and ran down a hallway. There were several staircases along the way, and eventually he came to a door that led outside, in back of the hotel.

The killer could have gone anywhere.

Deflated, he turned and walked back inside.

"What the hell happened to you?" Reed asked when Clint entered the lobby. By this time Clint had put the gun back into his belt, but he didn't bother hiding it behind him anymore.

He also realized that there was something wet on his forehead. He put his hand there, and it came away with blood. The stall must have hit him harder than he'd thought.

"Come with me," he said to Reed.

"Here," Reed said, handing him a handerkchief.

Clint thanked him and pressed the cloth to his bleeding head.

He showed the Inspector Jeffery, who was quite dead. They had to move the stall off of him to ascertain that much.

"Stabbed," Reed said. He was down on one knee and turned to look at Clint. "You must have almost caught him at it."

"He killed Jeffery because Jeffery saw him when he sent the champagne up."

"Which means he definitely must work for the hotel."

"The killer must also have killed Foxhall, the clerk from the store."

Reed stood up and said, "I agree."

"That means he's killed five people already: three women and two men. The men he seems to be killing out of what he feels is necessity."

"And the women?" Reed said.

Clint shrugged. "Maybe he just likes it."

Reed put his hand on Clint's shoulder and said, "Come on, let's see about getting you patched up."

THIRTY-FIVE

The hotel doctor patched Clint's forehead up in his office while Reed looked on.

He wasn't in a good mood.

"What do you mean by running into the lobby waving a gun?"

"I was chasing a killer."

"I just gave you back the gun this morning, and already you have to cause a stir with it. You scared people half to death."

Clint looked at Reed and said again, "I was chasing a killer."

"Stay still, please," the doctor said.

"Did you at least get a look at him?"

"No," Clint said. "It happened too fast."

"Damn it!"

They remained silent while the doctor finished bandaging Clint's head.

"It was a nasty cut, but you don't need stitches," the doctor said. "You might have a headache for a while. Take one of these if you do."

He gave Clint some white pills, which Clint had no intention of taking.

"Thank you, doctor. What do I owe you?"

163

"Not a farthing," the doctor said. "Compliments of the hotel."

"Thanks."

Clint stood up, and he and Reed left the office.

"I'm not angry at you," Reed finally said to Clint. "I'm angry at the killer for killing again, and I'm angry at myself for not being able to catch him."

"You'll catch him."

"How?"

"He must be in a near panic, now. He stepped up his timetable once, maybe because he felt we were getting close. Now I walk in on him while he's killing the bellboy. According to his own schedule, he's got two girls to go. He's got to step up his timetable again."

"You're right," Reed said. "I'll fill this hotel with my men."

"Well, don't make it so obvious."

"What do you mean?"

"If you fill the place up with men, and he notices them," Clint said, "he might go someplace else for his last two victims."

"Jesus," Reed said.

"What?"

"I just realized something."

"What?"

"He's off his timetable; that means he's no longer copying the killer in France."

"So?"

"So," Reed said sadly, "if he gets to five, who says he's going to stop there?"

THIRTY-SIX

The man was angry.

He was angry with Clint Adams, this legend of the American West, for walking in on him while he was taking care of Jeffery.

He was angry with himself for almost getting caught. That's what he got for killing men. He should stick to women, which meant he could no longer get cute, like sending the bottle of champagne up to the Swede's room. He could do nothing that would involve anyone else.

He couldn't kill Adams, then, because he wasn't going to kill any more men, but he knew that Adams was seeing Lesley Anne Collins. He had already chosen Lesley Anne as his last victim, and he now looked forward even more to killing her, because he knew what that would do to Clint Adams.

He closed his eyes for a moment and pressed his fingers against his temples in an attempt to calm himself, but he could not. There was only one thing that would calm him down.

He had to find his fourth victim.

Now!

• • •

Elise Montalbano worked for the Romero Weapons Manufacturing Company of Spain and was late getting to the expo. To avoid being caught entering late, she was going to try to get into the hotel by the back door.

Elise was only twenty-one, very slender and pretty. She had gotten this job because she spoke English well and had been thrilled because she had never been outside of Spain before. She had learned her English in school and had been very eager to try it out where English was the spoken language. So far she had been getting along very well.

Nervously she approached one of the hotel's back doors and reached for the handle. She pulled and found it locked. She was trying to decide whether she should try another door or just go in the front and apologize for being late. She didn't want to get fired, because she didn't know if the company would send her *back* to Spain if they fired her.

Then again, did she *want* to go back to Spain?

She turned to walk away from the door and walked into a man. "Oh!" she said, startled, but not at all frightened.

"Trying to get in through the back?"

"Yes, I was, but it is locked."

"Don't want anyone to know you're late, eh?" the man said with a knowing smile.

Shyly she said, "I—it is the first time."

"Well, come on," he said, reaching into his pocket. "I have a key. I'll let you in."

"Oh, how wonderful," she said, and turned to

face the door, waiting for him to open it.

She frowned when she felt the blue silk scarf wind itself around her neck.

She died puzzled, never even having time to become frightened.

THIRTY-SEVEN

By afternoon Reed had eleven men in and around the hotel, but his instructions were to keep a low profile. The men were dressed as waiters, bellboys, busboys, clerks, and the like.

Their job was to locate and stop the killer. While positioning themselves, one of them went out behind the hotel and found something.

Reed and Clint were in the dining room having coffee when Hyde-White and Standford both came hurrying in.

"Clint, there you are," Hyde-White said.

"We have been looking all over for you," said Standford.

"We need you downstairs."

"For what?" Clint said. "I think my part in this expo has been a bust, fellas."

"Not now," Standford said.

"What's so different about now?"

"You were seen this morning waving your gun around the lobby," Hyde-White said.

"And everyone heard you had a tussle with the killer," Standford said. "Everyone wants to talk to you now."

"You'll be a big hit with that bandage on your head."

"Look, I can't," Clint said.

"Why not?" Standford demanded.

"There's something more important I have to do."

"Look," Standford started. "We went out on a limb for you—"

"And I appreciate it, but this is important."

"Look—" Standford started.

"Gentlemen," Inspector Reed interrupted in his most official voice. "I'm afraid this man is in my custody."

"For what?" Hyde-White asked.

"Suspicion."

"Of what?" Standford asked.

Reed shrugged and said, "That's confidential."

Hyde-White looked at Clint and said, "Well, we tried to help you."

"I know you did."

"Come on," Standford said. "We have to get back downstairs."

When the partners left they passed one of Reed's officers on the way in.

"Inspector?" the policeman said, stopping at their table.

"Yes, Spikings. Sit down."

"Uh, sir, I have some bad news."

Reed closed his eyes and asked, "What is it?"

"The fourth girl," the man said. "We found her in the back of the hotel."

Reed brought his fist down on the table so hard

that he attracted the attention of everyone else in the room.

"Four down and one to go," Clint said. "He's really pushing it now."

Out back Reed and Clint stared down at the girl's body.

"This is really going to build his confidence, you know," Reed said.

"I think he did this before you placed your men in the hotel," Clint said. "But I think you're right. He's going to go after number five today or tonight."

"And I'm going to stop him!"

"He's got to be an employee of the hotel, Reed," Clint said. "That's why his victims have all come from the hotel. That's how he got into the Swede's room."

"Take care of her," Reed said to his men, and he and Clint went back inside.

"Wait a minute," Clint said, putting his hand on Reed's arm.

"What?"

"That first night," Clint said, "the killer had to have followed Harriet out of the hotel."

"So?"

"So, he would have had to go past the doorman, only he claimed he didn't see anyone."

"Then if he didn't see anyone . . ." Reed said.

Clint made a fist and punched at the air.

"It had to be him!"

• • •

The man felt invincible.

He knew that Scotland Yard had the hotel full of men. He knew because he recognized them as *not* being employees of the hotel.

Even though they were all there, he knew he was going to take his fifth victim right in their midst, and there was nothing they could do to stop him.

And after he had his fifth victim, why should he stop there?

"It's the only thing that makes sense," Clint said. "It must be the night doorman."

They went together to the manager's office, and the man stood up.

"This is terrible," he said. "Terrible for the hotel. Our business—"

"It's even more terrible for the people who were killed," Clint pointed out.

The man stopped short and then said, "Yes, of course. Can't you do something?"

"What is your night doorman's name?" Reed asked.

"The night doorman?" the manager said. "Saunders, Henry Saunders."

"Where does he live?"

"Why, he lives right here in the hotel," the manager said.

"*In* the hotel?" Clint asked. "Isn't that unusual?"

"He was hired last month and did not have a place to live. We have a few rooms we supply to employees until they can get settled."

"Where?" Reed demanded. "Where's his room?"

"On the second floor," the man said, looking puzzled. "Room 204. What is going on?"

Clint and Inspector Reed rushed from the room without answering him.

"Do you have your gun?" Reed asked.

Clint hesitated, then said, "Yes."

"Good!"

THIRTY-EIGHT

When they reached room 204 Reed flattened himself against the wall on one side, while Clint did the same on the other. Clint took out his gun, and they both listened at the door.

Clint motioned to Reed that he would kick the door open and go in first. It made sense, since he was the one who was armed.

Clint stood in front of the door, lifted his foot, and kicked the door just beneath the doorknob. There was a splintering of wood, and the door flew open. Clint moved quickly into the room, his gun held out in front of him.

It was a small room, and it was readily evident that it was empty.

"He's not here," Clint announced, slipping the gun into his belt.

Reed entered the room and looked around. There were bed sheets and clothes strewn everywhere.

"He's not very neat, is he?" Clint asked, but Reed was beyond humor.

"He's in the hotel somewhere," the inspector said, "stalking his next victim—but I swear he won't have her!"

"Well," said Clint, "we're not going to find him standing around here."

He left the room, assuming that Inspector Reed would be right behind him . . .

The man—the *killer*— moved down the hall as quietly as he could. He could hear the noise from the lobby: policemen mixing with guests and members of the expo.

The killer didn't care if he was caught—as long as it was after he had claimed his fifth victim.

Lesley Anne Collins.

When Clint and Reed reached the lobby they saw that all was in chaos.

Reed snagged one of his men and said, "What's going on?"

"Word has gotten out that there's a killer in the hotel, sir," the officer said.

"Jesus," Reed said. There were people all over the lobby. Some of them were heading for the front door, others were at the desk, probably demanding refunds.

"Get these people out of the lobby," Reed said. "Tell guests to go back to their rooms. Tell non-guests to go down to the rooms where the expo is being held."

Just then there was a shot from downstairs.

"What the hell was that?" Reed asked.

"If there's a panic," Clint said, "some people may be grabbing guns downstairs."

"Christ, that's just what we need. I'll have to get some men and go down there."

"Go ahead," Clint said. "I have to see someone."

"Who?"

"A woman," Clint said. "I want to let her know what's happening."

"All right," Reed said. "But be careful. Keep a sharp eye out."

Reed went one way, and Clint started toward the hall that led to Lesley's office.

Lesley Anne Collins was trying to concentrate on her work, but the racket outside was pulling her attention away from it. Finally she decided she had to see what was going on out there.

She stood up from her desk and stopped short, startled, when she saw the man in the doorway.

"Henry," she said, greeting Henry Saunders, the night doorman. "You startled me."

"I'm sorry, Miss Collins."

Saunders was a tall, thin man, who presented a mild-mannered appearance. She couldn't imagine what he was doing there because, to her best recollection, they had never exchanged more than two words.

"What can I do for you, Henry?" she asked. "And what is that infernal racket out there? Has the place gone crazy?"

Henry didn't answer.

"Henry? What is it? You look strange."

Saunders put his hand into his jacket pocket and said, "I have something for you, Miss Collins."

"Henry if this can wait until later—" she said, starting to walk past him. He put his hand against her breasts and pushed her back so hard she banged into the desk.

"Henry, what the—"

She stopped when she saw what Henry had taken out of his pocket. It was a scarf, a silk scarf of a brilliant, shocking yellow.

"Henry—"

Henry wrapped the scarf around his hands and said, "I have something for you, Miss Collins."

"Oh, God, Henry," she said, realizing that he was the killer. "No . . ."

THIRTY-NINE

Clint was walking down the hallway to Lesley's office, when he heard a strangled cry.

"Henry, no—"

"Lesley!" he shouted and ran down the hall.

When he got to the door he saw Lesley with a yellow scarf around her neck, and the night doorman, Saunders, standing behind her. Saunders was tightening the scarf around her throat, and she was virtually hanging from it, clawing at his hands.

"Let her go, Saunders!"

It was only then that Saunders noticed Clint, and the look on his face was one of extreme annoyance.

"Go away," he said. "I'm not finished yet. Get out of here!"

"You're finished, Henry," Clint said. He took his gun out of his belt and pointed it at the man. "Let her go . . . now."

Now Henry Saunders became indignant.

"You have no right to interfere. Get away!"

Clint thumbed back the hammer and said, "Let her go or you're dead."

Clint didn't know where it had come from, but suddenly there was a knife in the man's hand, and he had it pressed to Lesley's throat.

179

"I'm in charge here, do you understand?"

"Take it easy, Henry. There are Scotland Yard men all over the place."

"Do you think that matters? I'm leaving, and I'm taking her with me."

"I can't let you do that, Henry."

"I told you," Henry said, speaking slowly, as if addressing a child. "I . . . am . . . in . . . charge. Now put the gun down or I'll slit her throat."

"Clint—" Lesley croaked. Her eyes were filled with horror.

"All right," Clint said, pointing the gun up. "All right."

"That trash basket by the desk," Henry said. "Drop it in there."

Clint took one step to his left and dropped the gun into the basket with all the papers. It sat right on top, in plain sight.

"All right," Henry said. "Now back out the door and move toward the back."

"You can go out the front—"

"The front is full of people," Henry said. "Don't think you can fool me. Now move."

"I'm moving, Henry, but I'm not letting you out of the hotel with her. If you want her, you're going to have to kill me first."

"Clint, no—" Lesley started, but Henry pulled on the scarf and cut her off. He still had it around her neck, both ends held in one hand while the knife was held in the other.

"Back down the hall," Henry said.

Clint stepped out of the room and backed down

the hall. He probably could have made a run for it, but that wouldn't have done any good.

Henry Saunders stepped out in the hall with Lesley in front of him, between him and Clint. Clint saw Inspector Reed coming down the hall behind Henry, but Henry was already concentrating on two people and couldn't hear the third.

Reed moved down the hall at the same speed as Henry, Lesley, and Clint, and when he got to the office he looked inside. He stepped into the office then, out of Clint's sight, but was back momentarily —holding Clint's gun. It looked very foreign in the inspector's hand.

Clint hoped that Reed wasn't going to shoot Henry, because if the bullet traveled wrong it could go right through Henry and into Lesley—but he saw that that was exactly what Reed was going to do.

Reed held the gun ahead of him in both hands, and Clint shouted, "No, don't!"

Henry stopped, unsure as to what Clint was yelling about. Reed fired, and as he did Clint leaped forward and grabbed Lesley, batting away the knife that Saunders held in his hand.

The yellow silk scarf was taut in Henry's other hand, and Clint reached over and yanked it from him.

Henry had straightened up and was standing funny as Clint pulled Lesley to him. He put his arms around her and turned away to shield her in case Reed fired again.

There was no need to fire again, though. Henry opened his mouth to speak, still standing stiffly erect, and blood flowed over his bottom lip and down his chin.

"Don't fire again!" Clint shouted.

Reed lowered the gun as Henry fell forward, landing at Clint's feet. The knife was still held in his hand.

Reed came down the hall, a shocked look on his face.

"I killed him."

"You're lucky you didn't kill us all, you damn fool," Clint said. "That bullet could have gone right through him."

"Clint?" Lesley said, her voice very small and weak.

"It's all right now, honey," he said, speaking softly. "It's all over."

"I killed him," Reed said again.

"You sure did," Clint said, taking the gun from him.

"I think . . . I'm going to be sick."

"I would hope so," Clint said. "There's a trash basket in the office. Use that."

Reed turned, stumbled down the hall into the office, and could be heard retching.

"Come on, honey," Clint said to Lesley. "You're not going to want to go in there for a while."

FORTY

"When do you get over it?" Reed asked.

Clint and Inspector Reed were sitting in the hotel dining room the next morning, having coffee. In the corner Hyde-White and Standford were having breakfast—or staring at it. Their expo was over, because most of the people had checked out in the wake of the chaos that had taken place the day before.

The hotel itself would survive, but Hyde-White and Standford would have to think up another scheme to make up the money they had lost on this one—and that scheme would probably have to be illegal in order for them to recoup their losses.

They'd survive, though.

"When do you get over it?" Reed asked again.

Clint studied the inspector.

"You don't," he said finally. "You don't get over it, but you do learn to live with it."

"It might not even have been him I was shooting," Reed said. "It might have been *her*!"

"James," Clint said gently. "You're going to have to live with that, too."

Reed looked at Clint with haunted eyes and said, "I know, I know."

"Just remember," Clint said. "You saved Lesley's life yesterday."

"Sure," Reed said, "and I could just as easily have killed her if what you said was true."

"What did I say?"

"That the bullet could have gone right through him into her."

Clint made a face.

"Yeah, well, I said that in the heat of the moment."

"Was it true?"

"Uh, well, yeah, it was true enough, but the fact remains you caught the killer and saved her life."

"Yes," Reed said. "I'll hang onto that."

"You do that," Clint said, standing up. "You're good at what you do, Reed. Don't forget that, either."

"You going home tomorrow?" Reed asked, looking up at him.

"I've got a ship out in the morning."

"Well, I'll say good-bye now," Reed said, also standing.

They shook hands, and Reed left the dining room. Clint was about to leave, too, when George Cameron came in and spotted him.

"Clint!"

Clint saw he couldn't avoid the man, so he waited for him to reach him.

"I'm leaving now," George said, "and I'd like to have your answer."

"My answer?"

"Yes, about the gun, about naming it after you."

"Oh, that," Clint said. "Well, George, I don't really think I want to agree to that."

"But why?"

"The idea just flat out doesn't appeal to me, George," Clint said. "I'm sorry."

"But—"

Clint walked past him into lobby.

"I'll get in touch with you when we get back home!" Cameron called out to him, but Clint ignored him.

Clint went back up to his room to pack and leave. He hadn't seen or spoken to Lesley since she'd gone home after the previous day's experience, but he hoped to find her before the day was out.

He found her when he opened the door.

She was in his bed.

Naked.

"You could get fired for this, lady."

She sat up and let the sheet fall away from her lovely, naked breasts. She lifted her arms to him and said, "Then come and make it worth my while, mister."

Later, after they had both made it worth their while, he sat up in bed abruptly.

"What is it?' she asked.

"I just remembered my bet."

"What bet?"

He told her about the bet he'd made with his friend, Rick Hartman.

"I don't see where you lost the bet," she said.

"I stuck my nose in somebody else's business again."

"Whose?"

"Whose?" he said. "Yours, for one, and Inspector Reed's—"

"Who was the main suspect in the murders?"

"I was," he admitted.

"And whose business was it to clear you?"

He brightened and said, "Mine."

"See?" she said. "The only person's business you were looking after was your own."

"That's right," he said, lying back down next to her. "Now all I have to do is convince Rick of that."

She kissed him and said, "Let him try and prove otherwise."

Watch for

NEVADA DEATH TRAP

ninety-eighth in the exciting
GUNSMITH series

coming in February

J.R. ROBERTS
THE
GUNSMITH